Sean Patrick O'Mordha

A Pirate's Legacy:

Book III

CIC: Canary Island Commandos

A Pirate's Legacy:
CIC
(Canary Island Commandos)

Copyright © 2012 Sean Patrick O'Mordha

ISBN: 978-0-9829842-7-7

Cover Design © 2012 Bill H. Moore

Produced in the United Sates

Celtic Publications
Sparks, Nevada

Other novels by

Sean Patrick O'Mordha

A Pirate's Legacy: For Glory, Truth, and Treasure
+
A Pirate's Legacy: The Urchin Pirate
+
A Pirate's Legacy: CIC (Canary Island Commandos)
+
Incident at Beaver Creek
+
Death by TOP SECRET
+
For All Time and Eternity: Waters From the Deep
+
Man With No Name

For electronic versions:

Smashwords.com

For print versions:

www.oldguey.webs.com
www.celticpublications.xipherzero.net
www.amazon.com

Dedicated to:

Brianne Kjar

A wife, a mother, and an inspiration
to us all.

CONTENTS

Prologue

My 15th Century great grandfather, François Evreux, led two lives. In public spheres he was known as a successful and generous plantation owner. In other circles, he was the pirate, Dolphin. Equally successful in that occupation, he buried a number of treasures around the Caribbean containing far more than gold and jewels. According to his journal, from an archaeologist's view these chests contain treasures of incredible scientific and historical value. Knowing where they are located and not able to unearth them has been excruciatingly difficult. However, the time finally arrived that my team members in the CIA (Canary Island Archaeologists) acquired the necessary education and equipment to attempt recovery of what could be the greatest of all the hidden treasures, the Guadalupe del Mar. A minor inconvenience would be evading the Cuban military, the US Navy, and my sworn enemy, a member of the Spanish Mafia, who is also in the hunt – for the treasure and my head.

The summer of my thirty-fourth year, we decided to begin recovery operations for the del Mar. Pride of the Spanish treasure fleet, her huge belly held treasures stolen from the Mayan and Aztec civilizations destined for Spain to be melted down and turned into their own kind of gods. My ancestor attempted to capture her, but as the del Mar fled for safe haven at Baracoa on southeast end of Cuba, she was driven by the wind onto submerged, off-shore rocks and sank almost immediately. Those not going down with the ship were dashed against the rocky shore, leaving my ancestor the only one who knew the exact location of the wreck.

Of course, we weren't about to tell the Cubans. They would have plowed ahead, destroying any historical data and then melt the gold down to fatten already pompous posteriors while their people continue to struggle. To accomplish this mission, we decided to set up a base of operations on the Haitian coast opposite Cuba, in the very quiet cove of Bahie du Mole. That's where I met Momma Bearbear, matriarch of the Barber Clan and certified Haitian witch.

As work allows, we take our children on projects. Few pose any real danger, but if that seems possible, we leave them with a dotting grandpa, aunt, and an island load of cousins on our home island of El Hierro. That's where our daughter and twins remained during this adventure. Our twelve year-old son, François, who responds better to Delfin, came along as the recovery site was across the Windward Channel and he could remain safe at the Haitian base. Or so I thought.

I expected to spend the first week or so earning the trust of the Haitian locals. That occurred within the first hour when Momma Bearbear discovered our connection with Dolphin. Astonishingly, she knew as much about him as I. From that point, we were family.

Momma possessed a whimsical attitude, often alluding to certain historical information, withholding details in a tantalizing way until letting it pounce on us like a jaguar from an overhanging branch. A good example is the fourth day after our arrival when she dropped a bomb that sent our lives into a cartwheeling spin – even hers.

"On one of your very great grandpapa's voyages, he delivrie son of Tainos Indian chief from being main course at Carib banquet. Boy's uncle was spirit man. He make prophesy that some day to come all pirate friends will be one. For many jenerasyon we watch prophesy come true in yo bones."

"What do you mean, the bones?" Delfin asked.

"Right here, boy," she said, retrieving a round, black metal canister from a high shelf in her white-painted cupboards. Mumbling something in the Haitian-Creole dialect that strongly suggested an incantation, she removed the lid and let him look inside.

"What are those? Chicken bones?" he asked while wrinkling his nose.

"Oh, no, not chicken bones, boy. They right, middle bone of first finger. H-u-m-a-n finger bones," Mamma Bearbear replied, letting the word roll off her tongue as if they were some great delicacy.

Chapter 1

The Paparazzi

Leaving El Hierro and returning home in Nebraska after the first summer on that island was like stepping into a room and turning off the lights. The glitz, glamor, and celebrity status hadn't made it that far. However, as word of our exploits came to the surface my popularity index increased markedly, something not especially welcomed. Still somewhat socially retarded, anonymity continued to be a preference, but all of a sudden, strangers wanted to be best buds, which made me nervous. Despite the risk of being labeled a snob, I was selective about making friends, and didn't especially like crowds trying to schmooze their way into my sphere of comfort. Then they showed up – the paparazzi. At least I guessed that's what they were, guys lurking about at the darndest times and unsuspecting places to take my picture.

At first, giving them the slip became a game like the time Raul and a couple neighbor girls went to the lake. However, as we got within three blocks of home I spotted a white, step van parked on the opposite side of the street. I'd seen it before with a telephoto lens poking out the driver's window. With a disgusted grunt, I ignored whoever it was, but then got this funny tickle in the back of my head. I learned to recognize that as a warning something wasn't quite right. Abruptly changing directions, we avoided coming close and losing them, for a while at least.

Two weeks later our first year in high school started. Just my luck our elementary principal, Mr. Hellman, or as Raul and I referred to him, Mr. Yellman because he always yelled at us for something or the other, was the new principal. I thought to have ditched the guy upon graduating to middle school, but no, he transferred, too. I'm sure he missed the interaction and did it deliberately. Then there rose out of the thundering herd of freshmen a couple bullies with a small following attached with IQs barely allowing them to make it through gym class. As everyone civilly jostled for a place to fit into this microsociety, these guys tried to force themselves on people because they wouldn't fit in any hole, no matter how they were turned. Naturally, they made their presence known by targeting loners and those who acted "different."

A week into school, Mr. Churchill, the gym teacher, demonstrated a sadistic streak. He matched star bully Ronnie Barker and Jeremy Krum to wrestle. Barker tangled with Raul and me early on in grade school and lost. There was a monumental celebration when he didn't return for fourth grade, but here he was like a piece of cracked china no one wanted.

Always on the large size, Barker had expanded into something like a small gorilla with the same amount of hair. Jeremy didn't even have leg hair. A poster candidate for an old Charles Atlas bodybuilder ad – the one having sand kicked in his face – he was somewhat effeminate which put a bulls-eye on his back for the likes of Barker. Susceptible to being knocked down by a light breeze, Bradford took great pleasure tossing Jeremy around like a piece of luggage at an airport. When Mr. Churchill thought enough damaged was done and a silent message sent among anyone else who didn't measure up to "man" status, he called time. You could see Jeremy hurt and struggling not to cry.

Standing with both arms high in the air, Barker announced, "King of the hill."

"Not yet," I said quietly from my sitting position on the edge of the mat.

In first grade, I was one of those loners Barker picked on until Raul came on the scene and helped change my perspective. He showed me how to step up and be counted when called for. That's why Mr. Yellman always yelled at us. We didn't fight on school grounds after that first time, but he didn't like having pupils show up to school with fat lips and black eyes. After what happened on El Hierro during the summer, I was well-tempered, both physically and mentally.

Barker sneered, made his usual, insipid comments, and then with Mr. Churchill's whistle, lumbered toward me. Before anyone could gasp, I had him on the ground in a hammerlock, screaming at the top of his lungs.

"You ever do something like that to Jeremy again I'll break your arm in little pieces and serve it to you on a platter" I whispered in his cauliflower ear before releasing the hold. No, I didn't break it, but he did have it in a sling for a week because of a sprained tendon.

Mr. Yellman had me in his office with Mr. Churchill at his side, railing about what I had done, concluding with, "Do you understand me, young man!"

"Perfectly, sir. And I presume Mr. Churchill won't match the biggest brute in school against the smallest kid again in wrestling just as a warning to other kids that might be different, either." My mouth was want to run off on its own.

"You're suspended for one week!" Yellman yelled.

"Fine. And you won't mind if my lawyer has a talk with the school board about your treatment of gay students, will you?"

Mr. Churchill's satisfied smile disappeared like Mario Andretti around the last curve to the finish line. There had already been some unrest about targeting gay kids and they weren't interested reopening that can of worms.

Like I said, Barker had the intelligence of a rock so he and another rock thought to have some "fun" with Jeremy again. Raul finished off the friend and I followed through with my promise to Bradford. We might have been in super trouble if not for a bunch of girls with a massive dislike for Barker who stood for us. The rock did swing first and Papa Montoya was my attorney. A number of select people were more than tickled with my transfer to a private school a week after that incident.

While I couldn't be there for Jeremy, things worked out when football tryouts kicked off that spring. The skinny gay kid had one heck of a throwing arm earning him the quarterback spot, and the bully was a lineman assigned to protect him with every ounce of brawn musterable.

Actually, a transfer to Daryl Hopkins magnet school was a boon. First, it was within walking distance of home, and second, it had a merging swim team. To the coach, I was just another wannabe who showed out of nowhere at the East Lincoln Aquatics Club a week after practice started

"Show me what you can do. Give me a hundred meters," she said.

Mrs. Fletcher was in her second year coaching. She'd been a competitive swimmer in high school and college with a few medals and stuff, and dreams of seeing some of us be successful, too. Of course, with all the swimming she did, her body was well-toned, and in a bathing suit caused more than a few of us to have palpating hearts. Despite a pleasant disposition, we quickly learned she demanded and accepted nothing less than one-hundred per cent plus.

Without hesitation, I sprinted to the edge, dove in, and completed two laps, got out and stood in front of her with, "What else would you like?"

Her mouth slung open knowing that hadn't taken nearly as long as expected. An assistant came over and showed her a stopwatch. I leaned over and looked, too.

"Is that time okay?"

"The state record was just set at 45.08 seconds. You just did it in 51.7."

"I probably could go faster, if you'd like. Want me to try?"

She just looked at me before recouping enough to say, "We'll work on that."

I wasn't bragging. For a kid who spent most of the summer swimming with dolphins, I didn't feel like having pushed it. I never reset the state record, but did give it a nudge. For the moment, one could see visions of a state championship dancing in her sky blue eyes.

Moving to the diving platforms, she wanted to see how the new crop of swimmers handled height. The first springboard sat at one meter or a hair over thirty-nine inches above the water, the other at three meters. She had everyone start at one meter. There was a lot of feet first nose holding jumps and cannon balls. One hotshot did an honest to goodness forward one and half somersaults from the pike position. As it turned out, his dad was pursuing a swimming career through the kid, and they moved to town just before school started up. I just did a straight, headfirst dive.

Next, we moved to the three-meter board. It was more of the same, except the semi-pro did three and half somersaults. I restrained myself, keeping an eye on the next level. And then we climbed to the five meter platform. That separated the "men from the boys" so to speak. Some jumped or fell, but a significant number backed off. Those of us not intimidated graduated to the seven and a half meter platform. That's a scary twenty-five feet in the air if you haven't been there. Only two of us jumped as everyone else retreated to sanity. He did a very nice one and a half somersault in the straight position according to the coach. I walked to the edge, looked down, looked at the coach, shrugged, and jumped, again entering headfirst.

As we stood on the approach to the ten-meter platform my competitor said, "It's a long ways down there." He had a smug smile.

For the initiated, that was a good description. It's equivalent to jumping off a three-story building. I shrugged my shoulders and said, "I suppose."

He walked out, turned his back to the pool, and executed a decent two and a half somersaults in the pike position. I didn't know anything about scoring, but it looked impressive, punctuated by o-o-o's and ah-h-hs from far below. I walked out to the end and looked down thinking of my dolphin friends swimming back and forth waiting for me to join them. When I walked back, the kid looked up and grinned. If smug had a brother, his grin were twins. To everyone's surprise I ran full-bore, leaped into the air, arms spread to take flight, and yelled, "Ya-ah who-o-o." Doing a decent jack knife, I split the water, hardly disturbing the surface. Darn, if that didn't become my nickname from then on.

"You've been off a thirty meter platform before, huh?" the kid said while we showered.

"In all honesty, no. At my home in the Canary Islands I've got this rock hung out over the ocean. It's something over forty meters."

"That's over a hundred and thirty feet!"

"I think it's closer to 150 feet."

"That's impossible."

"Those guys in Acapulco jump that far."

I'd love to get him on the dragon's head. He'd eventually do it, of course, and become addicted, but it's scary hitting the water at about thirty-five miles an hour and shooting toward the bottom forty feet below the surface.

Despite making a few new, casual friends at Hopkins, my relationship with Raul didn't change. We still hung out when he wasn't preoccupied with some girl. You see, if a person steps back and takes a long look at him, it's understandable why he's so popular. I mean, geez! Here's this tall, physically put-together dude with long, raven black hair and eyes, and a perpetual tan courtesy of his Moorish heritage. And then there's the accent. He can speak better English than me, but chose not to because it caused girls to go glassy-eyed. When he pursued gymnastics and wore an ultra-tight leotard, they flocked to the stands like sparrows on a fence eyeing a bird feeder.

Spring came early that year and the first Saturday in May turned really nice, so we decided to spend the day at Holmes Lake. Raul invited Cherise, a ditsy brunet with the thought capacity of a loose cannon. I never understood what Raul saw in the girl other than she had big boobs. Her incessant giggling drove me nuts. At the lake, she didn't want to get her swimsuit wet, if those two pieces of anemic cloth pasted to her body could be called that. It was beyond me why anyone would go to a water activity and not get wet. I think Raul had the same thought as he spent a lot of time in the water while Cherise held down a beach towel and repeatedly lathered suntan lotion on her body in sensuous ways.

I invited Sandy who lived directly behind grandma's house on the next street. She was about as opposite as one could find from Cherise. She wore a one-piece suit, loved the water, was a dynamite volleyball player with a deadly spike, had a tan dark like mine, and didn't giggle. In lots of ways, Sandy reminded me of Concepción with long, reddish-brown hair tied in a ponytail. Having known her forever made it easy to be around her. She also spoke Spanish and just to tick Cherise off, we spoke it most of the time.

By noon we had tried to drown each other a couple dozen times, swam races, played a mayhem version of water polo, won four straight games of volleyball against some older kids, and ate a to-die-for lunch Sandy and Mrs. Montoya put together that morning. To top everything off I cued up some melodic, Spanish CD's, stretch out on a towel, and let my tired and well-fed body die.

Sandy lay on her towel a couple feet away while

Cherise was practically on top of Raul, ostensibly oiling him down with suntan lotion from foot to neck. Not that applying suntan lotion isn't a bad idea. We all had hints of pink around the edges, except of course for Cherise who looked like the inside of a Twinkie. My concern was the way she applied the cream and the way Raul was enjoying it. On our side of respectability, I applied some to the exposed, upper portion of Sandy's shoulders. It felt really weird doing that, but she had done it to my back. We did our own legs and front, thank you.

Late that afternoon we reluctantly gathered up to wander home. Cherise's mom picked her up because she was just too exhausted to walk all the way home, if eight blocks was all that much. We collectively turned down an invitation for a ride. The weather was still too nice to ride. I also got the distinct impression Raul had enough of Cherise.

As we escorted Sandy to her house, I felt a tickle on the back of my neck as if something were crawling over it. Leaving her house, we came back around the corner to head for Raul's home. The all too familiar little feet began a tap dance on the nape of my neck .

"Something wrong?" Raul asked as I rubbed the back of my head.

"Feels like something crawling on my neck." Raul was aware of the feeling I painfully became familiar with on El Hierro.

"I don't see anything. Want to make any bets it's that van down the street? Paparazzi." he said, casually indicating a nondescript, white panel truck parked at the curb on our side of the street just beyond the alley entrance ahead. Paparazzi had become a nuisance since returning and especially since the magazine article came out a month earlier about my adventures.

"No bets," I grumbled. I'd seen it frequently the past week hovering close to wherever I happened to be.

"Hello, boys."

"Hello, Mrs. Douglass," Raul responded to a neighborhood friend digging fertilizer around the numerous rose bushes in her front yard.

Mrs. Douglass is one of Grandma's genealogy colleagues whose house sits on the east side of our block next to the alley running behind Grandma's and the Montoya properties. She, Aunt Florence, and Grandma's relationship reaches back to high school days. Next to Grandma and Mrs. Montoya, she bakes the best pastries, but that wasn't the incentive to help do some yard work and shovel snow off her sidewalk. She is a sweet, old lady. Of course, we never said no to iced lemonade and ice cream rolls in July or warm cinnamon rolls and hot chocolate on a bitter cold, January day.

"Mrs. Douglass, don't turn around, but do you know how long that van up the street has been there?" She knew everything that happened in the neighborhood down to how many caterpillars crossed the street.

"They parked about twenty minutes ago. Nice looking young man, a little darker than you two. Kind of sexy-looking." She giggled. "He'd be more attractive if he didn't smoke. I'll bet he's paparazzi." She knew the problem I was having.

The itch got worse. "Do you mind if we go through your backyard so they don't know we used the alley?"

"Not at all, although I think they might be too busy to bother you in a few minutes."

"Why's that, Mrs. Douglass?" Raul asked.

"I called the police. Never can be too careful, you know," she said with an enduring twinkle in her eyes.

We said thanks and quick-stepped up the driveway until out of sight of the van, sprinted to the back fence, and over into Sandy's backyard. Peeking through the gate into the alley dividing the block, we saw a police cruiser conveniently parked behind the van. Knowing Grandma would be at her genealogy meeting until five, we continued up the alley to the gate leading into Raul's yard, and the smell of fresh-baked bread.

Before last summer, life was pretty low-key. In fact, life was so low key teachers had a hard time re-membering our names until well into the school year. We had mellowed by middle school so even the vice principal for discipline didn't know us. Upon return-ing from the Island, we all decided it best to not say a lot about inheriting a plantation and discovering my pirate ancestor's treasure right away, but the news media forced the issue. First on the scene, reporters from KOLN-TV, followed by reporters from the Jour-nal Star newspaper, with calls from talk shows hot on their heels, and then various magazines, and . . . the list grew exponentially. Papa Montoya pre-emptively arranged for a PR agency to handle the deluge. That helped except for the appearance of paparazzi. In my case it was nothing like the flockings around really famous people, just an individual photographer now and then. Secretly vane enough to enjoy the attention and becoming a bit of a show off, at first I'd give them some poses. After a time it became a nuisance as the time Grandma and I were shopping in preparation for our return to El Hierro.

Since last fall pant cuffs posted signs of ankle creeping and by spring looked like pedal pushers. A quick check on the kitchen wall chart pegged the top of my head at five foot, ten and a half inches. The first part of April, a month and a half before returning to the island, there was a long weekend off from school, a busy weekend. El Españia was throwing a big celebration for some members getting married. Without saying, I expected a request to perform the Chufla, and both Grandma and I feared the stretchy Flamingo trousers had already stretched about as far as we dare allow. The first afternoon of vacation, she hauled me to the Gateway Mall to buy clothes.

Knowing my quixotic tastes, she didn't exactly trust me to shop for regular clothes alone. She was right, but I wouldn't admit it then. While rummaging through more conservative selections and bored, several distractions raised their snake-like head. First was a girl about my age leading a pack of four giggling tagalongs.

"Aren't you the guy who discovered all that pirate treasure?" she asked, her face pink as a grapefruit, to which I replied in the affirmative. "Can I touch you?"

Rolling my eyes, I held out a hand. She tentatively reached out hers, but I got this whimsical notion, took her hand, and kissed it as had become my custom on the Island with older ladies. Her face turned darker pink while issuing another inane giggle. Her friends joined in so that it became a gaggle of giggles. At that moment a shaved head with camera attached popped over a clothes rack and flashed off a couple quick shots. Backing away to rejoin her groupies, they undertook a quick, squealing, giggling flight. Of course, it was a setup and I couldn't wait to see what the Enquirer or some teen mag would do with those pics.

"David, I want you to try on these trousers," Grandma said, obviously annoyed.

"Hey, paparazzi, I'm going into the dressing room. Wanna take pictures in there, too," I called out sarcastically.

"Yeah," came a reply as this guy extricated from his hiding place in the middle of a clothes rack.

"Not in your lifetime, baldy," Grandma countered, taking a step toward him.

I'm not sure if it was the fact she was a head taller, a lot broader, and equipped with a death ray scowl, or the store security moving in, but the character beat a hasty retreat as I disappeared into the dressing booth. Grandma took up position in front of the entrance and stood guard like one of those Buckingham Palace guards.

Stepping out of the fitting room, Grandma looked me up and down, spun me around, and approved by saying, "If you're done putting on elevation, they should last a while. You are too active for circular expansion like your grandfather Eben. It appears to be all clear, now. Go ahead and change back while I slip over to the lady's department."

Back in my original duds, I noticed a sale on walking shorts and detoured there a minute. That's when Barker and a couple guys from my old school showed up. I think he put himself to sleep every night thinking of how he'd get me alone someday. The bozos thought their dream had come true and started with the usual imbecilic insults. They weren't aware of Grandma until she came up on their backside like battleship approaching three rowboats.

"Do you have a problem, Mr. Barker?" she asked.

Barker, who perpetually mouthed off to teachers, obviously wanted to reply with some smart, derogatory remark, but again Grandma's mere countenance derailed pursuit of that venue. He'd been in her classroom six years before and withered like a white tomato on a droughted vine. About the same color, too.

"No, Mrs. Dolephene," he replied, cowering and quickly moving off.

Two weeks before school ended, as Papa Montoya drove me home from swimming practice he said, "The PR people have told me that a Spanish people magazine would like to do a photo-story about you. It is legitimate. He would follow you around for about four or five days taking pictures of the things you do."

"Let me think about it."

That evening before bed, I was finishing homework when the Captain appeared. Somehow, he knew when I wanted to talk to him, and I told him about the photo shoot.

"You are famous Francis, and good publicity could not hurt."

A week later Señor Cervantes sat across from me, Sandy, and Raul in grandma's living room to discuss how he would become a shadow and snap pictures of the things I did. As difficult as it might be, we were to totally ignore him.

At first it took some adjusting, but he was easy-going, personable, and generally unobtrusive. Eventually, I didn't even notice the camera clicking. He took pictures of me talking with friends, devouring a hamburger at a drive-in, dancing at El Espana, attending church, and playing with friends at the lake, sans Cherise thank heavens! Staying in the spare room at Grandma's he shot pictures from breakfast to bed-time.

Just before he wrapped up the assignment, I stuffed a spoonful of shredded wheat into my mouth and then asked, "Pablo, would you do me a favor?"

"I will try. What is it?"

"That van that's been following me around, the paparazzi?" He'd seen it, too. "I'd kinda like to turn the tables on them. Could you take a picture of them if they show up when we come home from school?"

"Of course. It might make an interesting sidebar."

Sure enough, the van was waiting, but this time at the curb on our side of the street. Pablo went ahead and just as I approached the vehicle, he turned and snapped a couple pics. When that happened, the van suddenly took off and disappeared, all the while that uneasy itch on my neck grew intense until the van was gone.

That evening Momma Montoya served up a farewell dinner for Pablo after which Papa broke out the guitar. With Sandy as my partner, we danced. She brought along a friend so Raul wouldn't have to dance with his mother. The next morning at breakfast, Pablo reached into his shirt pocket and handed me a couple photos.

"Here are your paparazzi friends in the van."

I laughed at the vision of them tearing off like spooked rabbits, and then stopped, staring at one of the photos intensely. It was blurred because the van moved pass Pablo so quickly.

"What's wrong?" Grandma asked.

"If I didn't know better, that looks like Fuentes in the passenger seat," I said.

Chapter 2

Home Again

Teachers in private schools are more stoked and creative as if fresh out of college, and pumped by equally enthusiastic students and administration. Activities we pursued made learning enjoyable and memorable, but nothing they did could take my mind from that last day of school when the building itself would exhale us in relief.

Each day closer to that moment became agonizingly slower than the one before as if life itself was a wheel about to come to a grinding stop before reaching the magical moment. The problem was knowing that within days after being jettisoned from the building I would be on a plane to El Hierro in the Canary Islands and reunited with my brother and sister, Alejandro and Concepción. During those last few days, I often caught myself staring blankly at the blackboard as if stranded in a time warp.

Grandma made flight reservations months in advance. I wanted to charter a plane, but she smiled, looked at me over the top of her wire glasses, and quietly said, "That is wasteful, Francis. Besides, don't you enjoy the attention the flight crew gives us?"

"I'll hire a flight crew," I replied with youthful excitement, having a teenage penchant for letting money burn a hole in my pocket.

"And what about the young girls on the commercial flight?" She chuckled and had her way, quietly teaching me yet another valuable lesson about the value of a dollar even if you literally have tons.

It wasn't as if she was poor. Like her sister, Aunt Florence, Grandma possessed a comfortable bank account, if a million dollars or so is any judge of comfort. Both widowed, the two ladies were habitually frugal, enjoying a simple life, and I do mean enjoy. Especially after retiring, nothing made them happier than genealogy work – and me. I never realized how my presence filled their hearts with joy until both were gone. Although my life has been richly rewarding and full, there will always been a hole without them.

With our flight to El Hierro arranged, it became a matter of counting down the time to departure, first months, then weeks, and finally that last day at school with its agonizingly slow hours dribbling to an even slower trickle of minutes. Of course, the teachers knew this and silently counted along, but the State Board of Education obviously had a work-aholic's brain fart, scheduling the last week with proficiency tests. Coming down to the last twenty-five questions on the last test on the last day I could have cared less and blazed through them. That probably was true salvation as I aced the ex-am. My problem with testing is to think too much about the question, attempting to cipher and se-cond-guess what is being asked. Finally, the last bell sounded and the halls erupted into a boister-ous tumult with the final, metallic slam of locker doors, and thundering feet out the front door. We were free, free at last!

That was the last Thursday of May and our plane was booked for departure on Monday. The excitement was nearly impossible to contain. The plan was for Momma Montoya and Raul to accom-pany us as far as Madrid for their annual family vis-it. Papa Montoya would join them three weeks lat-er. In order to prevent exploding, Sandy and some friends from school met at Holmes Lake where we picnicked, swam, and generally horsed around both Friday and Saturday. Sunday was reserved for church, of course, and final packing.

In that, I had packed a suitcase the week be-fore, taking only essentials with the expectation of buying clothes there. Grandma spent the evening closing down the computer system. Too excited to sit in front of the computer, I declared Genealogy would wait and headed to Raul's house. Papa Mon-toya engaged us in a spirited game of round-ball, two on one. I still don't know how he did it, but we had a heck of a time getting around, over, or through him. For a guy pushing forty something, he was amazing!

Finally, Momma Montoya called us to dinner. I was for loading into the Montoya family SUV and head for the 48th street Valentino's, not far from where we lived, thinking it would be a farewell meal neither Grandma or Momma Montoya had to fix. They wouldn't hear of it, and when the aromas began tickling my nose, I was not disappointed. Of course, Grandma was in the thick of the kitchen helping. Quickly washing up, Raul and I helped set food on the table. It was a marvelous meal after which us menfolk took over the kitchen. Raul cleared the table, Papa washed the dishes, I dried, and Raul put them away. In no time, we joined the Señoras in the front room. Shortly thereafter, the dancing began. At last! I was able to expend the energy that had built to an incredible pitch over the past weeks. At the conclusion I performed the Chufla.

Hearing that song the first time sparked a fire in my breast and instantly became my most favorite Flamenco. It's hard to resist joining in as the foot strikes the floor sounding like a heavy machine gun accompanied by hand claps. My style tended to be thunderous, making a statement accompanied by shouts of '*Ole*,' or '*Anda*,' or '*Alla*' from onlookers. Normally 6/8 time, Papa's fingers grazed the guitar strings with blurring dexterity, accelerating the tempo to dizzying speeds until I fell wasted onto the sofa at the last chord amid lots of laughter. It wasn't until years later I learned of his relationship to the flamenco guitarists Ramon and Carlos Montoya. He could have been a famous musician too, choosing to practice International Law with the same flamboyant adroitness.

Early the following morning we flew a charter to Omaha where the four of us caught a two-hour jaunt to Atlanta. While Raul and I explored the airport there waiting for our overseas flight, Grandma and Mama Montoya relaxed in the VIP lounge. Three hours later, we passed security for the nine-hour flight on Air France to Madrid arriving at 8:00 a.m. that next morning. Of course, Grandma was right. A chartered plane may have been faster, but small and not near as fun. Going first class made it possible to stretch out in the seat, walk about, and receive pampering by the flight crew. And, as she insinuated, a charter wouldn't have provided the opportunity to meet a couple cute girls who kept Raul and me awake the whole trip. Fourteen hours and exhausted, we touched down at Madrid-Barajas International. Primed to change planes and continue on, Grandma neglected to mention that we would stay over several days with Montoya's family to rest and adjust to all the time changes. After working through customs, a big group of cheering and waiving Montoyas met us in the lobby and kept us up another twelve hours before the two of us crashed.

Awake, sort of, the next day, Raul gave me the native's tour of Madrid. Thursday I was feeling more alert as while driven to a small community up the coast from Barcelona where the Montoya villa – more like a family timeshare – overlooked a beautiful, private beach where we spent some serious sand time regaining lost tans with his cousins until catching a Spanair flight Saturday morning from Barcelona to Tenerife.

My brain feeling clearer, the excitement level began rising as our Boeing-Douglas MD-87 began circling the island preparatory to landing. So far there had been a number of delightful surprises Grandma neglected to mention, each coming like a nearly endless string of Christmas presents.

Disembarking, we were greeted by none other than the lip-biting-beautiful lady who prosecuted Fuentes and his gang. Having moved up in government circles and hearing of our return, she eagerly took it upon herself to meet us in the terminal and provide a personal escort to the VIP lounge. Pretty as ever, she was still not married. How such an atrocity could happen was beyond me, as my adolescent brain secretly toyed with the hope she'd stay that way a few more years until I was eligible to consider matrimony. Seeming so interested in every humdrum thing I had done, it spurred further hope she might be interested in waiting for me, as well.

All too soon, the booming voice of Señor Gonzales rattled the great windows overlooking the tarmac and hills beyond. "Don Evreux!" Arms open wide as his grin, the bull of a man charged into the lounge to envelop me, before unexpectedly backing off. "I am so sorry, Don Evreux, one should never greet a marqués in such a *grosero* manner. I am sincerely apologetic."

I stared at him a moment before throwing my arms as far around my third cousin as they would go. "Yes, you should." His reciprocal hug nearly cut off breathing.

Disengaging a second time, there was a tear in one eye as he stepped to Grandma and kissed her hand. "Welcome back, Señora Dolephene."

"Ah-h, Don David, there is someone I want you to meet," Señora Alvarez-Rodriques said while looking beyond me to a debonair gentleman entering the lounge in Señor Gonzales' wake. "This is my *novia*, my fiancé, *Profesor* Victor Reyes."

Someone yelling "Earthquake!" would have had the same effect as the ceiling toppled on my swooning head. The storybook-handsome, Prince Charming as sculpted by Di Vinci shattered my adolescent dreams with one stroke of his chisel.

"It is an honor to make your acquaintance, Don Evreux," he said, shaking my hand. It was a firm, confident handshake.

"A pleasure Señor Reyes," I answered, remembering my manners, but not cheerfully.

"Congratulations. When is the wedding?" Grandma asked.

"In five weeks," he answered.

"We would be honored to have your presence," the Señorita said.

"We would be delighted."

"Victorio is the Assistant Director of Education for all the Islands."

"Your generous donations have furthered education not only on El Hierro, but throughout the Canaries as well because of the increase in tourism money. I have been very busy keeping up with all the changes."

"Sounds as if that will keep you away from home a lot." I replied, still pouting.

"Oh, that should not be a problem," my heart-throb replied. "We are not so spread out that Victorio cannot be home almost every night, especially when the children arrive."

Children! That bucket of Gatorade doused my last dying hopes. I was sixteen, barely out of puberty, and still in high school. How could I possibly compete with that? Having that dream trampled into the concrete floor, I acquired lead shoes as Señor Gonzales escorted grandma and me out to his new airplane and packed us in. Posterity had arrived for him, as well. Unfortunately, they didn't make cockpits any larger as he had to wiggle into his seat like before. The only difference was that I sat as co-pilot and even handled the controls a little once we made altitude. Learning to fly became another item on my "to do" list.

Setting down at Valverde, we walked into the terminal while Señor Gonzales insisted on handling the baggage. Just like last year, there stood Papa Vasquez, as dashing as ever – tall, lean, the neatly-trimmed mustache as thick and black as remembered, ruffled white shirt overlain by dark gray waist jacket with silver-trim, form-fitted trousers, and calf-high boots. A knot tightened in my throat upon seeing the man who had become like a second father like Señor Montoya. I will always miss my dad, remembering it took two great men to replace him.

Next to him were Alejandro and Concepción, more than my very best friends, they had become my brother and sister. Attired much like his father, Alejandro had gotten taller, too. Concepción may have added some height, but now stood several inches shorter than her twin, the long, wavy, dark brown hair tied in a ponytail. My mouth went dry.

When we first met last year, they dutifully acknowledged our arrival before hauling off to fetch the luggage. This year as we stepped through the double doors into the terminal, Concepción squealed and outran our brother, throwing arms around my neck and planting a kiss on my cheek. Two paces later Alejandro enveloped us both in a group hug. Out of the corner of one eye, I saw Papa Vasquez take Grandma's hand and kiss it.

From the airport, we drove straight to Aunt Herminia's villa overlooking Valverde and another mushy reunion, and then to the back veranda where more extended family waited (which seems to be most of Valverde's residents and half the island). Yes, it was nice to be home, but by eight Grandma was exhausted and excused herself. I continued with the party until eleven when everyone began leaving. Still wound tighter than a new mainspring, I had plenty of energy left which meant a stroll through the streets to the disco and another welcome home party.

Alejandro became more conservative in dress after Concepción's joke last year. Only the top two buttons of his shirt were undone so to not cover a crucifix. His black shorts were much less tight and below the knees. However, for the disco I was back into walking shorts and sandals. Feeling less inhibited and more frisky, I left the top three buttons of the ruffled shirt undone to show off the old key that had opened the treasure chests to this new life. Concepción cocked her head and closed one eye when I presented myself before leaving.

Knowing what she was thinking, I leaned close to her ear and whispered, "No good, sis, I never swim naked."

She stepped back, stared at me with mock surprise before displaying that faint, upward curl at the corners of her generous mouth and a twinkle in those soft, puppy eyes that precursored trouble. I swallowed. Once again, when I should have kept my big mouth shut, it flapped like a loosened sail in the wind. I'd set her on a quest and she would think of something – eventually. Unless vigilant, I was doomed.

We danced and partied until four that morning before staggering back up to the villa where I collapsed into bed until nearly noon. Coming into the kitchen to find something to munch on, I looked a sight. Aunt Herminia glanced up from her lunch preparations and snickered. I had passed a full-length mirror on the way down. Approximating a puppy-ravaged chew toy, my hair was a gargoyled mess, my eyes bloodshot and drooping. Still in pajamas, they hung on me like limp rags as my bare feet shuffled across the tiled floor. Fortunately, the family wing had a separate entrance to the kitchen by going around the back on the outside balcony and down the curved stairs; otherwise her guests might have overdosed from laughter.

"It is so good to have you home," she said with another hug, trying to keep from flouring me with her hands.

Aunt Herminia is a loving, Panda-like woman, soft-spoken, deliberate in her actions, with a huge smile and greater laugh. Pictures of her younger years revealed a thin, beautiful woman. The body had filled out a bit, but the long, wavy, light brown hair hadn't changed. Bound in a knot on the back of her head, a small, vertical comb adorned with polished red stones rose up from it, a gift I sent at Christmas. They were rubies collected during a Scouting trip to northern Idaho several years BT, Before Treasure, as I often refer to time now.

It never failed to amaze me how such a warm, kind, loving person would not garner the attention of suitors. She did, of course, but remained widowed, like Papa Vasquez, for nearly twelve years. I liked the smell of her perfume. It was the same Concepción used. On the other hand, I hadn't showered yet and self-conscious that I may not smell quite so wonderful after working up a sweat at the disco.

"Did you have a good time last night?"

"Oh, yes," I replied with a yawn.

"Good. Sit down. I'll fix you something."

"Don't go to any extra work. I'll just . . ."

"Nonsense. Growing children need three meals a day," she said, just like Grandma. If anyone else referred to me as a child, my response would not have been friendly. I was sixteen. I was a man – well, sort of.

"Where is Grandma?"

"Oh, she and my brother went to the museum. Now, tell me all about your year."

I'd sent regular eMails, and letters, and pictures, and talked to them on the phone, but she wanted to hear it all again in person, interjecting a string of penetrating questions until the last bite of breakfast/lunch had been devoured. Then Alejandro appeared, as sleepy and disheveled as me. Without complaint, Aunt Herminia fixed him something to eat, too. When Concepción bound in from the guest patio she was the picture of a saint, neatly attired in lime green pedal pushers, a cream-colored blouse, bright blue neckerchief, and hair tied back. Her energy must have been the catalyst my body needed to rev up into high gear, because ten seconds after she appeared I felt ready to face the world.

"Good morning sleepy heads," she chirped, giving the two of us a quick kiss on the cheek. "Can I help, Aunt Herminia?"

"Have our guests arrived for lunch?"

"Yes. Cousin Hernandez just arrived from the morning tour. They are cleaning up."

"Good. Get them seated and set out the fruit plates. The sandwiches are in the cooler."

"I'll get out of the way and take a shower," I said, becoming more self-conscious that paying guests seeing someone pad around in pajamas at noon might not give a good impression. I wasn't worried in the slightest what people thought of me. I didn't want to create a bad reputation for Aunt's villa, which was really a bed and breakfast for tourists.

The Captain built the place as a residence Valverde while governor. That it mirrored Casa de St. Nazaire was no surprise. Drawings in the museum depict a smaller place with additions over the centuries expanding it to the current large, two-story structure capable of housing a lot of people. However, about the only things remaining from the original construction were the beautiful marble fountain in the courtyard and the eight-foot perimeter stone wall. Remodeling, refurbishing, and the second story addition changed the appearance so that he might not recognize it if he came back from where dead people were supposed to be and walked in today. Of course, he already did that last year, so he knew, making the thought rhetoric.

There are twelve large guest rooms and four suites on two floors. Until refurbishing was complete, Grandma and I occupied two of the upstairs guest rooms. The rest of the family had additional rooms along the back. There are three sets of large, communal bathrooms on the second floor and a large family room directly above the public dining room with its own large, covered patio deck. Many quiet evenings were spent there or lounging in the family garden also at the rear. An ornate, curved stone staircase connects the family rooms with the garden, and the eight foot, stone wall on either side retains privacy.

At the back of the lower level is the public dining room opening onto a huge, tiled patio. Next to it is the kitchen and then the private family dining area. A sitting room is located across the patio entrance from the public dining room. Except for an office, the rest of the lower level contains three guest rooms, three suites, and two sets of communal bathrooms. The broad covered veranda with balcony above encircle the entire building, and a thick, rock wall encompasses the entire property except at the rear where it shrinks to four feet so not to obscure the mountain vistas beyond.

That the Captain loved the outdoors was obvious from the design. Windows are seldom shuttered except during really nasty storms. Otherwise, the perennially mild climate encourages one to enjoy the comfortable breeze.

Alejandro staggered into the bathroom just as I was stepping out of the shower at the family end of the villa. He still wasn't completely awake as he stumbled into the shower. Towel wrapped around my waist, I was trying to wrestle a couple kinks out of my hair with a brush when there came a light knock on the door just before it cracked open. It was Concepción.

"Is sleepy head in the shower?" she whispered.

"Yes," I responded, suspecting she was up to no good, again.

Pushing past, she slipped up to the curtain, reached in, and fled. She hadn't quite cleared the door when Alejandro let fly a piercing scream. She'd turned off the hot water!

"That should wake him up," she tossed over her shoulder with an effervescent cackle and disappearing down the courtyard stairs.

I was standing mouth open when the curtain flew back and my brother launched an IBM glare. In defense, I pointed wordlessly at the open door as an older couple exited their room at the far end of the balcony and stared at a kid in a towel with his mouth open, arm stretched out pointing an accusing finger in their direction, and another trying to cover himself with a shower curtain.

"Concepción!" Alejandro yelled. "Why didn't you stop her?"

"I didn't know what she was going to do," I squeaked in defense.

"You know you will be next."

"And you will know what she is up to and stop her."

He looked at me with a wicked gleam in his eyes, "Not likely."

Yes, it was good to be home.

Chapter 3

An Old Friend

The stopover in Spain was for a number of reasons. Primarily Grandma wanted to start working off the jet lag. Also, this was a great opportunity to meet some of the people we'd spoken to on the phone. The day following our arrival on the island was pretty quiet, spent recovering from all the partying and cruising about town. The third morning home we climbed into the back of Papa Vasquez's new minibus. Grandma, on the other hand looked and acted a bit off her usual pace as she sat in the front. Still, an air of excitement moved us forward as Papa Vasquez headed out for a lazy afternoon drive to Casa de St. Nazaire.

It was still a narrow, twisty, dusty road, however there were marked changes upon the land. The fallow but weedy fields were now plowed and sprouting crops. The trimmed vineyards no longer looking like a Medusa thrown to the wind. That meant return of the grapes to produce El Hierro's own brand of preserves based on a unique, family recipe Grandma discovered while rummaging around in historical research. That proved a better money-maker than wine, something everyone produced. Besides, I was still trying to decipher the secret, family wine formula hidden in the other family journals. Elsewhere, bands of sheep grazed over the rolling, grassy hills, lazing in the mild sunlight. Suddenly the VW swerved.

"Sorry," Papa Vasquez apologized, "I thought that lizard was going to step in front of us."

We three looked at each other remembering another time when that happened and turned in unison to gaze out the back window. Of course, everything was obscured by a dense cloud of dust. Unpleasant memories surfaced, but now we could laugh at some of them.

"Not getting any funny feelings to turn back, are you?" Concepción asked.

"No. Not this time," I snickered softly, not mentioning a sporadic tingling at the back of my head that had pestered me since February and shifting into a higher gear a week before leaving Lincoln. Most of the time, I chalked it up to the excitement of returning to what I began to consider my real home.

The first time it happened, Raul, a couple of our girlfriends, and I took a long detour to have a milkshake at Burger King after school. As we left, I had a feeling like someone was staring at us. I casually looked around, but didn't see anything except some cars, vans, and a few pedestrians. It happened off and on after that, often turning out to be a wanna-be paparazzi.

For a while it became a game. Upon spying them, I'd wave or put an arm around one of the girls or Raul—my weird sense of humor. Sharon got into the thing big time. She got caught more than once reading a teen mag in class and knew the kind of pics they wanted. One Saturday as we headed into a movie theater she conned me into allowing her to kiss my cheek. Oh, that wasn't good enough for me. She was the first girl I kissed full on the lips in public. That not only made paparazzi's day, but a fat bonus. Grandma and Momma Montoya never saw that publication, not that I was embarrassed. I really enjoyed that kiss. I kept it from them to avoid a lecture. I knew what they'd say. Besides, Papa Montoya said enough.

Several weeks after the mag hit the stands, Raul and I stopped at his office while window-shopping with some girls and paparazzi. Always the gentleman, Papa stood and shook each one's hand as we introduced them.

"I hope you left your checkbook at home," he teased.

"Just my weekly allowance," I said. Twenty bucks wasn't that much and most of it went for lunches at school.

"Here," he said, digging out a twenty from his wallet. "The deli on the corner has the best hot chocolate. Have them dash a bit of peppermint in it. Oh, and by the way, be mindful of those photographers following you. You have more than one reputation to protect." With that, he pushed a copy of that particular teen magazine to our side of the big desk as he sat down.

Sharon's face flushed as we quickly turned and left. I knew exactly how he came by that thing. The coy smile was plastered all over his secretary's face. After that, public relations were delegated to at most holding hands, and not with just one girl. When we left the office building that day the stalking photographer got a great shot of me holding hands with Sharon and another girl on either side. Raul held hands with a girl he was going fairly steady with. While there would be no more public kissing shots, that didn't mean lip-locking stopped completely. It was just more private. Well, most of the time. There was this one time at the lake in May. The guy had one heck of a telephoto, but fortunately Raul and his girl sufficiently blocked the view to identify anyone, and I wasn't with Sharon.

As the van broke from the trees, Papa surprised everyone by mashing the accelerator to the floor. The bumpy, rock ford had been replaced by a concrete so that two, arching plumes of water erupted either side of the van causing us to lurch forward as if a big hand tried to stop us, but no jarring bumps.

"How do you like what I had put in?" he said while laughing.

"Great," I answered trying to reclaim my seat, not having refastened my seatbelt when we turned to look out the back of the van moments earlier.

"Yes. Much smoother, and a good way to clean

the undercarriage," he said proudly.

The expression on Concepción's face was enough to know that was a total surprise. Papa was not given to sudden, impulsive behavior. Always very conservative and proper befitting his position as Curator of El Hierro's museum and its priceless pirate treasure, this was as big a transformation in him as had occurred to the plantation. However, this was only a fleeting sample to be visited later, in private with close family.

The wall of water parted like the opening of a sparkling, white curtain revealing Casa de St. Nazaire majestically growing from the volcanic cliff. Its beauty literally left me breathless. Under Papa's watchful eyes, my extended Island family restored the impressive mansion to its original splendor, carefully following drawings from the museum archives and the Captain's journal. Intruding vegetation was gone and the landscape neatly manicured. A new, slate roof adorned its crown. Exterior wood trim was replaced and the whole given a new coat of stucco and fresh, white and dark gray paint making it glow against the black, volcanic rock from which it extended. The dark green trees along the far, south side and attending slope appeared as a muffler. Fences along the circular drive sweeping around the front had been completely rebuilt and painted white. Even the original garden had been restored. A stout, wood fence encircled the perimeter as it had during Don Miguel's time. Not much was needed to restore the swimming/bathing pool except thinning the masking vegetation. Ensuing Evreux dons tweaked the place over the centuries with their personal touches and I was no exception with the installation of solar electricity and plumbing. Other than that, the place looked much as the day Don Miguel disappeared.

Remembering the difficulty my ancestor had keeping the garden weed-free, I was surprised to see no weeds, and remarked about that as we got out of the van.

"Oh, Alejandro and I come here at least once a week to do that. Hassan would have wanted that," Concepción replied.

"What do you mean wanted," Alejandro whispered. "He nearly kicked my butt when I objected." Then smiling said, "It has been fun, though. When we get through we go to the ocean or hot pool."

"Hassan has been visiting you guys?"

"Yes," Concepción replied.

"Interesting. I didn't think he had to do repentance."

"I think he's trying to help the Captain, too," Alejandro suggested. "Kind of repayment for what he did, you know, in Africa."

Inside the hacienda once barren rooms had been cleared to the studs, electricity and phone lines installed, and then re-plastered in the original antique texture style, including the original colors revealed during renovation. Handmade antiques and period furniture from Spain graced the rooms. Stopping just inside the entry beneath a majestic, wrought iron chandelier with realistic, electric candles, I stopped to stare at the staircase sweeping down from the second floor.

"What are you looking at?" Grandma asked as I seemed transfixed.

"It's so beautiful, just the way the Captain would have had it, isn't it?"

"Yes," Papa replied almost reverently. "I researched the era very carefully as you asked. You will have to tell me some time how you discovered those historical archives in Spain with such marvelous information."

"David is very proficient at research on the computer," Grandma explained. Neither would have understood how much came from the Captain.

"You should be able to move in next week if you like. Let me show you the rest of the house," he said, guiding the others around some canvas, paint buckets, and ladders.

"Go ahead. I'll catch up," I said, continuing to gaze at the top of the staircase, secretly wishing to see the Captain's ghost once again.

As the others disappeared across the courtyard into the kitchen and less formal dining area at the rear, I looked into what had been the Captain's study off to the left of the entry. That was the room Salvadore had thought to catch Concepción and me, but instead ended up putting a hole in the wall with his head. All evidence of that incident was gone, replaced by a small, writing desk, two lounge chairs, and shelves holding period books and charts.

Turning, I was about to join the others when movement caught my attention. Looking toward the second floor there he was, attired in a ruffled shirt open to reveal the medallion on his brown chest, striped trousers, and knee-high, black boots. A wide smile spread the thick, black beard encircling his mouth as he strode down each step until coming to stand directly in front of me.

"Welcome back, Francis."

"It's been awhile. Good to see you again, sir."

"The people have done a fine job here. Thank you."

"Is this the way it looked, when you lived here?"

"No. Better. I like the improvements."

I smiled.

"Will you turn it into a tourist museum now?"

"No, sir. This will be my home."

He smiled approvingly. "It will be good to hear the laughter of children within these walls again."

I choked. "That'll be a while."

"Time will tell. I was your age when Jean-Paul was born."

"It's a lot different today."

"Really? Such things happen with kissing, you know."

"Francis," Grandma called out, "You must see the kitchen. It's beautiful."

"You better catch up with the others. I shall see you again."

Joining the family in the kitchen, I was impressed how all the modern conveniences were deftly hidden to retain the room's charm of olden days. The one difference was the entrance to the cave. A heavy wood, arched door replaced the secret cupboard entrance. That's how it had been originally before Don Miguel's grandfather made the change and closed it off with a secret door, something that forgotten by everyone except the inheriting descendant, which explained how Don Miguel could disappear for centuries.

With expansion and addition of the second story, much of the original cabin the Captain built became one large room for parties. Those things would happen again, although I wasn't sure he would appreciate some of today's music. However, I planned to limit the sounds to more traditional renditions, which only seemed fitting for the atmosphere. The second level was given to bedrooms; the forefront being the Captain's which had a set of French doors leading to a covered balcony over the front veranda, both of which wrapped around the three exposed sides. This allowed windows to be open except during the harshest storms.

The remainder of the second story held a number of smaller rooms, which had been for the children, and a special, larger one for guests. That was where Grandma would stay. I planned to use one of the small rooms, but when we did move in, I found all my stuff put in the front bedroom.

"Some old guy told me to put it there," one of our younger cousins explained. "He's in there. Take it up with him."

The Captain was standing on the balcony, hands clasped behind his back, puffing on a long-stem pipe, obviously enjoying watching the activity below.

"Cousin Alvarez said you told him to put my stuff in here," I said.

"This is the master's bedroom. Yes."

"This is your room. So, where are you going to stay?" I quipped.

"Right here."

"There's only one bed."

"Don't worry. I don't snore. Not like you, anyway."

I was growing accustomed to having him pop in and out of my life since last summer, but hadn't seen him since just before Thanksgiving. Becoming reunited was great, but still, I wasn't so sure about sharing a bed with a ghost. My face must have reflected that feeling as he turned, looked at me, and began to laugh.

"I haven't slept in over 400 years, Francis. You shall have the bed to yourself."

"Just out of curiosity, what do you do when you're not . . . well, when I don't see you?"

"Go for walks or read. You've greatly improved the library. Thank you."

"We can go on the Internet and order more, if you'd like."

"I've already done that. The first shipment should arrive soon."

Good thing I found the treasure. A few days later $5,000 worth of books arrived, but hey, it is his money.

That first night at Casa de St. Nazaire I awoke and through sleepy eyes saw the faint image of the Captain sitting in his chair on the balcony reading a book by moon light. At least when in that room, I never felt safer or slept better.

Other than adding electricity and running water, the only other major change to the house was conversion of a large downstairs storage closet and an upstairs child's room to bathrooms. Chamber pots are for appearances only, and so was the outhouse, although there was one—for appearances. Completion of these facilities delayed moving in until the week after our arrival on El Hierro. That contributed to the problem that befell us.

Completing Papa's tour, we stepped back onto the front veranda. It was very different from when Fuentes strung Alejandro up by the ankles to torture him with a lit cigar in an attempt to force us to reveal the location of the family treasure. Sanded and painted a dark green with white trim, it now sheltered wicker seats and tables. These Papa and Grandma occupied while Alejandro retrieved a snack from the bus.

"There is something I have not told you," Papa started. He looked serious. "Fuentes escaped from prison several weeks ago. The authorities are certain he is no longer in Spain."

I told him about Pablos's paparazzi pic that looked like him. We said no more as the food arrived and I had better things to think about.

As we scarfed down Concepción's sandwiches, sipped lemonade, and chatted, my mind wondered back to when the Captain must have sat on this very porch with his wife and family or guests and did much the same thing. How slower and deliberate life must have been, able to take time to enjoy life. I looked up at the tips of the pine trees swaying in the gentle breeze, felt an occasional caress of that breeze as it slipped down through the branches, and across the meadow laid out before us. No TV, no car noise, nothing but the stillness of nature. A very different life. Yet, youthful energy refused to allow time to sit very long. Shifting my attention toward the stream I spotted one of the great lizards perched on a flat rock surveying its territory as its ancestors had done for centuries.

"How's the swimming hole?" I asked.

"Much the same as when your ancestor lived," Papa Vasquez answered. "I had a man dredge accumulated silt and repair the dam. It is at least a meter deeper. There are towels in the car."

Claiming them, we sprinted through the deep grass toward the curtain of trees the Captain planted to give his wife and daughters privacy when they bathed. Sis was fast, but I determined to outrun her leaving Alejandro behind. Closing on the stand of trees we spotted a wide, groomed path making a figure "S", providing easy access and still maintain privacy from the hacienda and outbuildings. The Captain's bathing pool provided ample space for horseplay and a large, grassy area on the other side to lie in the sun to dry. I managed a final spurt and reached the rock-lined pool ahead of sis.

The lizard stared at us from its rocky throne, obviously bemused by such strange behavior as we drove through the trees to the water's edge. I was first to throw off my clothes and dive in, quickly followed by Concepción. Remembering our first swim last summer, I had a suit under the Bermudas. Alejandro held back.

"Not joining us?" I called to him from the middle

of the pond.

"I bet he didn't bring a swimsuit," Concepción teased.

"I do not want to become sterile," he countered, rehearsing Grandma's lecture from last year. "And you should be concerned, too, Brother."

"I am, but I'm not planning to wear it all day and night like you did."

"Come in," his sister coaxed. "You do not need one with us."

"I do not swim like Concepción. Not anymore."

"Don't tell me you're not wearing anything beneath those precious soccer shorts of yours," she continued to tease. She really was like a puppy with a bone that way.

"That is none of your business, but yes I am."

"Hey, they'll work just as well," I called back from the far side. "Worked for me last year when you set me up."

He remained rather resolute about not joining us, but eventually the lure of our fun was too great to resist. After a few minutes I saw him kick off his tennie-runners, slip out of the T-shirt and shorts, and jump in. I don't know what his hang-up was. The dark, plaid boxers were perfectly acceptable. We played for nearly an hour before sloshing ashore and spreading out on the sweet-smelling grass to let the warm breeze and sun dry us off. It was heaven. Stepping from the water, our brother cast his eyes about in search of spies while quickly donning the bright blue shorts before joining us.

It was a relief knowing the paparazzi wouldn't be

slinking about. Grandma had told Aunt Herminia who passed the word to the right ears. Any of them showing up on El Hierro would find life an exceptional challenge. There was freedom of the press on El Hierro, but not as liberal as back in the States, especially if a family member was involved who didn't want the attention.

This was the first we three had any real time alone together since arriving. We talked about what happened over the winter months. Neither could phantom the cold and snow I spoke of. Enveloped by perpetual spring on El Hierro, they had not experienced such climatological delights.

After a while the conversation trickled down until my eyes closed. Just on the verge of falling asleep, a rustling noise drew my head up. Her Majesty, the lizard, had left the throne rock to lumber across the meadow not ten feet away. Stopping a moment, its tongue flicked several times as it stared a long time before lumbering off.

"Nosy beast. Had to see what we're up to," Concepción suggested as she pulled a brush through her sparkling hair.

"Better than a real chaperon," Alejandro said.

Now awake, I sat cross-legged and asked, "So how are the burns? They giving you any problems?"

"They're okay. Just small scars," Alejandro replied pointing to the one on his side, a light-colored circle on his brown skin about a half inch in diameter. "I'm lucky he wasn't smoking one of those big things."

"It gives him something to brag about to the girls. Of course, he doesn't show the ones on his legs.

They'd like to see the one on the inside. It is much bigger and quite impressive," Concepción teased.

"This one on my side is enough to get the attention I deserve."

"Never give up, do you?" I said to her.

"No. Not as long as he's my brother, and I will discover something about you in due time."

"Well, I hate to let you and all the girls down, but I've seen the other scars and they're really nothing more than light-colored blotches. The one on his side is actually the most impressive," I lied. "And, you will not live long enough to discover something about me," I countered, once more opening my big mouth when it should have stayed close.

Concepción feigned a pout, but there was a faint gleam in her big, dark eyes. "Want to untangle your hair while it's wet?" she asked, handing me the brush.

Ever since Aunt Florences' imbecilic son teased me about how my ears stuck out, I stopped going to the barber. Grandma didn't like it long, but understood and stopped harassing me. While that solved one problem, another cropped up. I was lousy managing a hairbrush. It always got snarled in the curls instigating a frustrating struggle. Sis moved to sit cross-legged behind me, pressing her knees against my back, taking the brush, and set to work.

"You have such beautiful hair," she said softly.

A tickle slithered down my back as I countered, "It's a devil to keep. One of these days I'm going to cut it all off or braid it into dread locks."

"Oh, no. Don't do that. I have some conditioner that will help keep it from tangling so badly, and if you tie it into a ponytail it will be just fine."

Alejandro looked on and rolled his eyes.

"Conditioner? "I said. "That's girl stuff."

"But if it helps who would know," she countered, "unless someone shot off their big mouth." She launched a lethal stare at her brother.

With a shrug of agreement I said, "The Captain did wear a ponytail."

"Yes. You could have one on either side," Alejandro quipped.

"I wish I had a piece of string," she said, ignoring him.

"I've got the leather cord holding the key."

Slipping the key from around my neck, I removed it from the cord and relocated it to the gold neck chain. I had been intending to do that for some time. Concepción took the cord and cut it with Alejandro's pocket knife, and then brushing the mass to the nape, she tied it off, braiding the rest and tying off the tip.

"You know," said Alejandro more seriously, "That's exactly how the Captain wears his hair in that painting we found in the cave. If you could grow a beard you really would be a dead ringer for him."

Chapter 4

A Date – Old Style

"Ah, there you are," Papa Vasquez called from the other side of the pond. "We should be heading back. Your aunt is planning a special meal and we don't want to be late."

Walking across the rock dam so only our feet got wet, we joined him and Grandma.

"Your hair looks very nice, David," Papa said.

"Ever since he started to let it grow long, I suggested he do that, but he said it would make him look like a girl," Grandma said as we gathered up our things and headed back to the van.

"Why'd you think tying your hair back would make you look like a girl?" Concepción asked.

"I dunno," I replied, feeling a little embarrassed.

"Do you want me to undo it?"

"No. No. It's fine."

"Are you sure? I don't want you to be embarrassed because of something I did."

"You couldn't do that. It was just a stupid male thing. I forgot the Captain wore it that way, and what's good enough for him is good enough for me."

"It is very becoming, Davina," Alejandro cracked.

"Watch it, Bro, or I won't warn you next time she comes in to turn off the hot water."

Reluctantly leaving Casa de St. Nazaire, we returned to the villa shortly after six. Rosa and Adalina, two fourth cousins our age, were helping as the last guests finished supper. That gave us time for a quick shower, something that surprised all three adults – quick that is. Teenage boys seldom take showers less than 30 minutes, but we were done in under five each. It also took Concepción by surprise, too. The door was locked as well.

"What on earth!" Grandma said as our sister's scream reverberated throughout the hacienda and several blocks beyond.

Alejandro appeared, but only I noticed he came from a lower level where the utility controls were located.

"Perhaps a gap in the hot water," he explained, taking a seat next to me, struggling to contain an evil grin.

"Oh, my! I must have cousin Bennie look into that. That will never do for our guests," Aunt

Herminia said.

When Concepción stomped onto the veranda the daggers coming from her eyes had us dead, but we both held up our hands to proclaim innocence. I, at least, was telling the truth only because of being unfamiliar with the system. Still, hair slightly wet and without makeup, she was attractive, more so when her anger was hotter than a downtown Lincoln street in July because that gave her smooth, brown cheeks a reddish blush. That tingling revisited the back of my head.

The meal was out of sight. Some of it prepared ahead by Concepción. As I was learning, she had become as good a cook as Aunt Herminia. As a matter of fact, I had better rephrase that. Neither was a cook, someone who just prepares food, they were chefs, one who creates wondrous culinary delights. This meal was one of those delights.

A meal is always a social event, especially the evening one. This one started with anchovies cured in vinegar, olive oil, garlic and baked, red bell peppers. The main course was *Paella*, a brilliant yellow, Valencia rice dish with slivered pork and shrimp. Piled in the middle of the table was hot, fresh, crackly bread and olive oil. White *Penedes cava* wine washed it all down. The crowning coup de grâce to my voracious appetite was *Manzanas Asada*, apples that have been cored and then stuffed with butter, sugar, brandied raisins, and baked.

"Oh, I nearly forgot, the Governor's secretary

called while you were away," Aunt Herminia announced as we men began to clean the table.

"Boggues isn't still here?" I asked, sounding disdainful.

"Oh, no. He left before Christmas. We have a new governor. A nice man," Papa explained.

"Of course, you would consider him nice. He's a nephew," Aunt Herminia teased. "Anyway, he has invited you to a reception to celebrate your return."

"Oh, my goodness, not again," Grandma said. "When?"

"A week from this Sunday evening."

"Oh, good," she sighed.

The last time had been a 24 hour notice. This invitation gave us adequate time to prepare.

"No problem. Grandma came prepared this time," I said.

"I hope you will wear that dress you had last year," Papa suggested.

"If you'd like."

This was getting a little thick, so cut in, "Isn't it taboo for girls to wear the same thing more than once."

"No one will remember. You were the center of attraction," Grandma answered. "A few accessories and it will be different."

"I remember," Papa answered. "You were ravishing."

"I can't wear the same stuff. Kinda outgrown them, but I got a tie-dyed shirt and some Hawaiian shorts," I interjected getting the expected response - lots of 'are you crazy?' stares.

"Back to the clothing shop," Alejandro announced.

"Is that pretty girl still there?"

"Kessare?"

"Yes."

"Can we bring guests to the reception?"

"Oh, I don't think she would go without her husband," Concepción said casually.

To say the least I felt shot down the rest of the evening. So far, everyone I had a crush on had gotten themselves married. The only remedy was a dose of disco, which had the ability to evaporate all but the worst funk, and maybe I'd find a date there.

We hadn't gone shopping or done laundry yet, so by this time the only thing clean was a T-shirt and pair of walking shorts. Wanting to wear long trousers, the only thing available were those worn to the reception last year. They were great for dancing. The problem being that they had also shrunk while packed in a box so the cuffs were several inches above the heel, but I figured to just stuff them into my boots. The waist had shrunk, too. Although made of a stretchy material, fastening the top button was still a serious challenge. After the third try, I sucked in my gut really hard and hopped around a couple times.

Buttoning the fly was easier, but there was no chance of sagging, as if I wanted to. That fashion trend wasn't really appealing. Sure, there are lots of colorful boxers and it seems a shame to hide

them, but sagging? The only reason for such behavior must be a subconscious wish one's pants
will fall down in a crowd of girls as a conversation
starter. Grandma suggested the manufacturers
promoted the trend to display the wide, elastic
waistband with their brand name in bold letters.

"They should lower their outlandish prices if
they want to advertise," Grandma said.

Standing in front of the full-length mirror, I
appraised the reflection. Wavy locks swept back
into the pony tail, white shirt undone to the
fourth button – to show off the neat gold chain
found among the treasures and now holding the
key – tight trousers a bit more revealing that I
wanted, and new boots – soft and danceable. I
hated giving up the original pair, but they had
shrunk too. Handmade, these were a gift from the
Montoyas' as we prepared to attend the local Festival de Jerez, a flamenco celebration the Lincoln
Spanish group holds each March.

When Grandma had me enrolled in the magnet school, Momma Montoya thought it would be
good for Raul as well. We didn't hang much during
the day, having a different class schedule and circle of girlfriends, but both participated on the
soccer team after which we walked home together, and hung together at either house doing
homework and nibbling snacks. Appearing at the
Montoya house almost every Saturday for dinner
and dancing after a full day of activities was a giv-
en. Upon returning to Lincoln after last year's adventure, I had more confidence and looked for-

ward to frequent weekends at El España. Besides being able to stay out until one in the morning and on one occasion until three – with adult approval – there were a couple girls there I really liked. The lateness of the parties would have never happened if not chaperoned, but what does that count for? I scoffed at that as a silly, Old World aberration.

On El Hierro we didn't need chaperons and staying out late was acceptable – not that Grandma didn't have something to say about the nocturnal hours; however I quickly discovered not every night. The biggest objection came from my body. Despite trying to maximize time while on El Hierro, functioning on three or four hours of sleep became an anchor leaving me sluggish and dulling enjoyment.

Transportation became the other obstacle to overcome. I had a learner's permit in the States and would get a driver's license upon returning, but couldn't drive on El Hierro. Alejandro wasn't supposed to drive, either, but most of the police were relatives and didn't say a whole lot so long as he behaved himself. My solution was to import three, 50 cc scooters a month before arriving. They weren't a Ferrari, but enough to enjoy the wind in my face and the sense of freedom. However, going to the disco was best done on foot so to sample some of the street vendors' treats, soak in the ambiance, and chat with friends.

The Governor's reception was decidedly different this time. It was great fun and far more relaxing compared to the starchy, formal thing last summer. The gentleman with the pointy beard who thundered our arrival with the gold staff even smiled and winked discretely. Of the many people I met last year, I recognized faces, but not their names. Once again, the chefs prepared a luscious meal. The belated birthday cake with sixteen candles melt in my mouth, the happy birthday song became boisterous, and my speech very polished. Of course, Papa and I worked on it ahead of time to convey my sincere love of the island and the people.

Governor Vicenzo Almeria was barely in his thirties and proving to be a capable administrator. Having a degree in political administration from the Universidad Compultense de Madrid, one of the oldest universities in the world, and experience in administration, certainly helped. Far from being self-aggrandizing as Boggues had been, Cousin Vicenzo was modest, relaxed, and funny. I have yet to meet someone with such a repertory of jokes. I darn near choked several times when he delivered a punch line to what I thought was a serious statement.

The meal lasted nearly two hours, although it didn't seem that long. Punctuated by searching questions, unlike last year, Señor Almeria wanted to know about America, specifically about growing up in Nebraska. Finally, it was time for dancing, and again, things were much different from last year. I wasn't nearly so shy as girls began lining up, but made it a point to dance with Governor's wife first. Much like Señora de Hernandez, Boggues' neglected wife, Señora Almeria was light as a balloon her feet and graceful as a swan. My waltz was adequate thanks to Grandma's tutelage.

Turning to greet the third girl on the docket, I stopped cold. It was Isabella Calderõn, the Minister of Finance's gangly daughter, but one heck of a dancer. As usual, she had hung in the shadows so I missed seeing her until now, and probably would not have seen her at all except for Señor Calderõn escorting her to where I stood next to the alcohol-free punch bowl.

Giving a courtly bow, I took her hand and kissed it. "Señorita Calderõn, what a pleasure to see you. I thought you had not come," I said, kissing the back of her hand under the eagle eye of Señora Calderõn standing several feet away.

"You have been very busy."

"I would not have been so distracted had I seen you earlier."

Okay, this is not your typical teenager's exchange, but then, this is not the environment of a typical teenager. The vocabulary and mannerisms are dipolar to "real" life. The first time, last year, the Captain sort of entered my head and put the right words into my mouth, a necessary, stopgap measure. Since then, there had been time for formal tutoring by my ghostly ancestor until I felt capable of cruising solo in the world of nobility, not that I wanted to, but when one is a marqués, some choices become limited.

Taking Isabella's dainty hand, I escorted her

to the dance floor as a waltz began. The first time we danced last year we were both stiff as Cousin Juan's staff, and it took a bit to loosen up, but this time we were both more relaxed, and I sensed a modicum of comfort in her. She was still a bit homely, with a longish, narrow face, and an equally narrow nose overhanging pinched lips, but Isabella had filled out some since last year, absorbing a few of the severe lines. However, beneath the surface was something very appealing. Being with her again felt nice. That must have become apparent as we danced several more times that evening concluding with a special request to repeat the flamenco of last year. Out of necessity, I toned my more acrobatic parts down for fear the trouser seams were already unduly strained, ready to burst their captivity.

Having such a good time, I was oblivious to time as the two of us stood talking near the never-empty punch bowl. She possessed a delicately alluring voice I really liked and continued plying her with questions about life in Spain where she attended school so to hear more of it. However, all good things must come to an end – thanks to adults – no matter how over-indulgent Señor Calderõn might be, Señora Calderõn was on top of things.

"I am sorry to interrupt, Don Evreux, but it is time we must leave. My body is not as youthful and is becoming obstinate about wishing to retire." The gentleman was inebriated, but not nearly as much as last year. His doctor had a few very stern words about altering his consumption.

Of course, I wanted to bid him good night and say that I would see the Señorita home, but knew better and controlled the impulse. Such an offer would fly like a lead cannonball with the Señora . She was old school, as in mulishly maintaining antiquated social conventions, and being so brazen would certainly jeopardize any future meetings.

Taking her hand, I leaned forward and kissed it, lingering a bit to enjoy the fragrance of the perfume, and then my mouth did something very brash. "Could we have lunch tomorrow?" I asked, somewhat haltingly, fearful of rejection, not that I hadn't encountered "no" from other girls.

"I would love to. How about coming to our villa, say around noon?"

"Noon it is." This time I really wasn't sorry my mouth shot ahead of my brains, which would have convinced itself such a meeting was out of the question.

This was one appointment to which I was prompt, presenting myself attired in a pair of light gray slacks and white shirt with only the top button undone so the gold chain would be barely visible beneath the collar. A black, waist jacket complimented my flat-brimmed Cordobes. That was the result of a quick trip to Kessare's shop that morning for some expert clothing advice. What to expect, do, and say was a bonus from the proprietor as usual.

Mouth-dry nervous and quivering slightly, I rode the dark blue scooter toward the Calderõn villa, that paranoid feeling of being watched adding to the discomfort. Of course, people were watching. After all, the American marqués was dressed to the hilt and heading toward one of the prominent families on the Island. Girls – old, young, married, single – always stopped to stare at the rich American. The feeling of being watched had to be reckoned with as long as I lived on El Hierro or anywhere else. Among close family I could be plain David, but outside that comfortable setting I was Don Francis Dolephene-Evreux, the Marqués Evreux, owner of Casa de St. Nazaire, and filthy rich patron of El Hierro.

Arriving at the Calderõn villa, a very starchy gentleman took my hat before escorting me to the sitting room off one side of the massive entry. Isabella was seated, her back toward me, playing a minute on the piano. I really don't care for classical stuff, but seeing her long, slender fingers tripping lightly over the black and white keys was enchanting. In fact, the whole scene was captivating, as if having been transported hundreds of years back in time – the room's deportment of lace and silks, and antique furniture, the music, the aroma of fresh flowers, the girl in a long, pearly-white dress seated at a piano, a servant hovering close to attend to whatever our needs. I silently hoped the Captain would be somewhere close, not that I wanted or needed his help, but so he could enjoy a slice of what had been his life.

"Don Evreux, it is so good to see you again," the Señora said gracefully gliding into the room, ramrod straight as always.

Taking the lady's hand, I bowed, and kissed it. "You are even more beautiful in the sunlight, Señora de la Barca."

She became absolutely radiant as I made a mental note to thank the Captain for that line, not that it was a lie. She was a very attractive woman for her age. "I am honored at having been invited."

Realizing I had arrived, Isabella stopped playing and stood. I took her hand and likewise bowed and kissed it. "Please, play some more. The song is beautiful." That was not a lie, either.

She blushed and resumed her seat as the Señora as I sat on one of several elegantly upholstered chairs by a polished wood coffee table, and sipped tea served by an ever-present attendant. Completing the minute, Isabella joined us for cordial conversation. In reality, the meeting was stiff and formal because of her mother's presence. I could tell Isabella was equally uneasy with the situation. Lunch was served on the patio overlooking the ocean off in the distance. The tension didn't ease as I continually fretted saying the wrong thing or worse, spilling something. It's tough being a teenager not yet in full control.

"These are very good," I complimented Señora de la Barca, referring to the finger sandwiches.

"Isabella is responsible. She made them herself," her mother bragged. "Well, if you will excuse me. I remember how important time is to young people," she said, and then left, however, not far.

It was not 'proper' for young people our age to be alone without supervision.

"Custom can be very confining," Isabella said softly.

"It sure can. Is that why I never see you at the disco?"

"Would you attend with your mother or aunt less than two paces away?"

"No."

Alone, sort of, we spent an enjoyable afternoon talking on the patio, and playing several games of dominoes. At my request, she played some Spanish music on the piano before taking a stroll in the spacious flower garden. Her mother was discrete, but never out of sight.

I silently debated much of the afternoon about asking for another date. Being in her presence was very pleasant, so as the visit came to an end I all but blurted out, "Would you like to go to the beach tomorrow?" holding out little hope she would accept.

"I would love to. It is one of my most favorite things," she almost squealed with excitement while desperately trying to retain proper deportment, "But, you will need to ask mother."

That was no problem. Full of confidence, I broached the invitation, inviting them both for an outing on the morrow.

"I am terribly sorry, Don Evreux, but I must decline the invitation, as alluring as it sounds. However, Isabella's Aunt Nelida would be available to accompany you."

"Wonderful. I'll stop by about eleven. We can have a picnic lunch as well. This time I cook."

A scooter can't float along the street, but this one felt as if it did as I headed back to Aunt Herminia's, wondering at what my mouth had just gotten me into. That feeling of being in danger tickled my spine. Me, cook? In the kitchen I was as dead as Charlie Tuna in a can.

As Concepción came to the rescue to help put together a great picnic she said, "I hope you aren't planning to wear those swimming trunks from the other day?"

"What's wrong with them?"

"The color. They make you look like a tourist, not like a Don on his outing with a person like Isabella."

It was also back to my clothing adviser on what a fashionable Don would wear in such an occasion. The last thing I wanted was to show up looking like a hick. My mistake was taking Sis.

Chapter 5

Beach Fashion

"Hello, Kessare," Concepción called out as we passed beneath the tinkling doorbell of the clothing shop that evening. "David has a hot date with Isabella Calderõn at the beach tomorrow."

"It is not a hot date. I'm taking a friend to the beach," I corrected, but that objection was a lost cause as the two plowed on. Girls!

"He needs a swim suit that is more fashionable than those things," she continued pointing to my top-of-the-calf Bermudas.

"I have a perfectly good swimsuit," I protested, wondering why I let her come along, except she invited herself and dragged me here.

"If you want to look like a blazing Picasso," she correctly responded. She was right, of course. The color or rather colors of the suit I wore at the hacienda weren't exactly as conservative as would be appropriate for this sort of outing.

"Something like this," I said holding up a pair of burgundy, mid-thigh shorts.

"Oh, that will not do. Not for a don," Concepción said. "No European in their right mind would wear such a thing, especially nobility." My eyes rolled up. "That is for the tourists. Exactly what you need over here." Stepping to the back wall she shuffled through some cellophane packages in a cubby, one of many. "Here we are. Size 30."

I looked at the package with the picture of a muscled stud barely covered by something a lot shorter than I'd only recently gotten used to. A wrinkled nose as if smelling rotten meat indicated I didn't like it.

"Let me see," Concepción said taking it from my hands and holding at my hips. "This might work."

"Oh, I don't . . ."

Of course she was teasing me to the hilt and I played right into her hilarity.

"You are perfectly correct," Concepción said at my hesitancy. "This is for children and old people. This is what you should wear," and held up another package.

My response was strangled into a broken squeak, but basically was an emphatic, "No!"

"Well, thongs are all the rage on the Mediterranean beaches, and we are seeing more of them here," Kessare agreed.

"No!" I squeaked, and then cleared my throat, trying to sound calmer. "I mean, really, that's not me. I don't have the body . . ."

"Oh, Don David, I disagree. So many of those who wear a thong do not have the body for it, that is true, but you . . .. Believe me, I know men, and you have the perfect body. You could easily be the model for this label," Kessare said. The problem with her reply? She was sincere.

"And you would not have but to do a little waxing," Concepción continued rowing for all she was worth.

"Waxing! Ah, no. I'll take this one," I choked, referring to the bikini with a three inch side.

"Better try it on, just to be sure it fits." Concepción said.

"It'll fit. How much? Never mind. Just put in on my account. Well, thanks girls. I gotta go." I swore to hear Concepción's cackle a hundred yards away.

The street crowds had to wonder at my red face. Hopefully, they'd pass it off as a sunburn. It didn't help matters when I bumped into two natty-dressed Italians who had recently arrived and were staying at the villa. They acted as if about to say something, but I excused myself and hurried off through the throng of people. Concepción had almost succeeded in "getting me." I'd have to be doubly cautious with her help for this outing, and then conceded that she may have succeeded, at least with the first part of her warped plan.

Back at the villa I sat on the edge of the bed staring at the new purchase. There was more package than contents. I couldn't wear something like that in public, but I couldn't wear my rainbow suit or Bermudas, either. That other thing was definitely out of the question. Thongs! They may have been invented

75,000 years ago in Africa, and popular in Japan for 2000 years, and is what people wear at the beaches now, but no thank you. I rapidly consoled myself to look like a complete retard in "sensible" swim wear.

Opening the package, I shook out the piece of Spandex material. The Brazil style suit was solid royal blue with deep yellow trim that could be reversed to yellow with a blue trim. The draw string waist was a plus. It could be cinched up tight and have no fear of losing it as happened last year. Migrating from knee-length to a square cut swimsuit with an eight-inch side was difficult at first, but Raul wore them, and after a couple trips to the lake, I gave them no more thought. These were cut to a three-inch side seam with a low rise to reveal a lot more. Eventually, slipping out of my clothes, I pulled it on and stood in front of the mirror. I was covered, barely, bare being the operative word. As for waxing, what was there to wax? Unlike Alejandro who had sprouted leg hair and a dark shadow from his belly button to disappear beneath the belt line, and an emerging tuft in the middle of his chest, the best manliness I could show was light-colored fuzz between knee and ankle.

"If you have dreams of being a woolly mammoth, I regret to say our family history does not give much hope of such happening," the captain said one Sunday as I was checking for facial hair in the mirror.

"Hey, brother," Alejandro said as he came into the room through the balcony door. "Whoa! Where'd you get that?"

"I let Concepción set me up."

"You knew it would happen. How did she do it?"

"I've got a date with Isabella at the beach tomorrow and didn't think my swimsuit would really work. I didn't want to show up looking like a florescent billboard. She agreed and dragged me to Kessare's. I just wanted one like I wore at the hacienda, but a solid color, something conservative. Kessare said this was all the rage on European beaches. Concepción wanted me to buy a thong. Somehow, I left with this."

"A thong might be super good to attract the girls, but this is more modest."

"Modest! I'm practically naked."

"You are fine. Actually, it looks very good on you," he consoled, and then draped over the arms of the over-stuffed chair to continue reading a book he carried. "How serious are you with Isabella?"

"We're just friends. She's a nice girl beneath all that stuffy, Old World veneer her mother imposes."

"Really?"

Arriving at the Calderon villa promptly at eleven, Isabella was waiting, contrary to what Kessare had confided during another shopping stop. It wasn't a trade secret, girls planned their appearance for after the date arrives and waited a time. The reasoning is pure female and escapes comprehension. I surmised Isabella rarely, if ever, had been on a date and wasn't about to delay this one. Okay, she wasn't the most glamorous girl in town, but something behind those soft, brown eyes was attractive and stimulating.

Decked out in solid beige Bermudas, light blue sport shirt, and sandals, I was nervous as a cat in a dog pound and getting more so as their family limo neared the beach. After setting up her Aunt's lounger under an enormous umbrella, Isabella's duenna settled her large frame in for the duration. She had a romance novel, but most of her reading would be over the top through telescopic bifocals. That made me even more nervous. What would she say when I removed my Bermudas to display the swim suite everyone insisted was appropriate. I thoroughly believed Concepción had set me up with the old bait and switch trick.

Spreading separate towels on the sand next to her aunt's umbrella, I just couldn't expose myself, and then Isabella removed her skirt and blouse. She was wearing a two-piece bikini! I swallowed the knot suddenly congealing in my throat. Beneath all that fashionable clothing her body wasn't as skinny as imagined. She really had a nice figure! Smooth, flawless, light olive brown, curved as if by a potter's hand. The shape of her face and hands were totally misleading.

"Let's go for a swim," she said.

Just then Concepción walked up. I should have known she couldn't stay away and not savor her revenge.

"Hi," she called out cheerfully, an Asian guy in tow.

"Hello, Concepción," Isabella greeted equally cheerful.

"This is Dòngbin Ling. I just love saying that. It's so musical. He just arrived from England on holiday. Ling is his first name. It means pure and virtuous. Dòngbin means a guest in a cave, so it all means a guest in a cave who is pure and virtuous."

Ling was in his late teens, early twenties, my height, with broad shoulders, deep chest, smooth, muscled, coppery brown skin. He looked to be athletic. I was right on with that. By Concepción's crowing, he was on one of the Edinburgh University rowing crews that took second at the Torpids bumping race at Oxford in March. Moussed coal black hair, sparkling black eyes, infectious smile, damn! Could anyone that looked like that be pure and virtuous?

"Sure he is," I grumbled to myself.

The girls giggled. Why do they always giggle? Ling smiled politely and rolled his eyes.

"Good day. You can call me Josh," he said in passable Spanish, reaching out to offer a very firm handshake. "It's very nice to meet you."

I resented the way sis hung on him, not sure why, but determined to keep an eye on the situation.

"We are just going for a swim. Will you join us?" Isabella asked.

Now that was just great! Isabella just offered Concepción a front row seat to my humiliation.

"We don't want to intrude."

"Oh, please. We will have so much fun, and David has prepared a huge lunch, more than we three could possible eat."

That explained what I considered excess food Sis packed.

"Well, okay," she replied, seeming to be genuinely reluctant before spreading their towels next to ours.

In seconds she and Ling, or Josh, peeled off their outer garments. She was wearing a two-piece bikini, too, and the Adonis Chinaman from England was barely covered by a real thong, making me feel as overdressed as a Polar Bear on a nudist beach. With a

"Come on," they raced into the surf.

"Are you wearing those?" Isabella asked.

Taking a deep breath, I pulled my walking shorts off, tossed them with the shirt and sunglasses onto the towel, and made a beeline for the water. Once safely covered by the incoming tide, I felt more at ease, but as we swam and frolicked, I began noticing every male on the beach from two up wore exactly the same style I had – or less. At Raul's family condo, we were on a private beach, so this was my introduction to public, European beach fashion.

Shedding feelings of self-consciousness were still not easy, and nagged me as we exited the water for some lunch. Josh and the girls quickly curled cross-legged on their towels to dive into the picnic basket. I casually draped a small towel around my waist. Concepción cast a questioning glance in my direction, but continued girl chatter with Isabella.

"You're going to school in England?" I asked in English, trying to be sociable.

"Yes. I am studying Classical Archaeology at Edinburgh." His English was impeccable with a slight Scottish accent.

"This may sound like a dumb question, but were you born in China?"

"No. My ancestor came to England in 1867 as an envoy from China. His youngest son accompanied him. He was seventeen. He fell in love with a servant girl. She became pregnant. There were words between father and son, and when the father returned to China, he remained in England. They married, but had no money, and he had few skills except for translating which became a valuable asset to the merchants trading with China. He had several sons whose descendants continue to this day in that endeavor. My great-grandfather joined the faculty at the University of Edinburgh as a lecturer in the Chinese language. My family has been associated with that institution ever since. My father is a lecturer of Oriental and Middle East history. His hobby has been Mediterranean archaeology with ties to the Orient. I want to make that a career."

"No kidding! I've become really interested in archaeology this past year." The ice was broken as we became busily engaged in conversation as the girls chattered on about their own thing.

"Actually, my travel here is two-fold. I want to enjoy some warmth and thaw out a bit. It has been exceptionally cold in the UK this year. I also want to visit the museum. I understand it has the most outstanding collection of pirate artifacts in the world with links to the Orient."

"Did you say you are interested in Papa's museum?" Concepción cut in.

"Your father runs the museum?"

Señor Vasquez is the curator," Isabella said. "It has become a very good museum under his direction, and then David and Concepción found the treasure. It is now very famous."

"You two are the ones who found the pirate treasure?" he broke into a wide-eyed grin.

"Not without help from their brother," Alejandro interjected as he joined us, a girl on each arm. He was wearing the burgundy, square-cut suit I originally wanted to buy at Kessare's. The girls were also in two-piece bikinis, severely stretched to their limits.

Isabella's duenna couldn't have been more pleased as the one-on-one date suddenly swelled into a group event. I was worried that would be a put-off for Isabella, but she obviously began having a great time as we talked, swam, and played Frisbee until Aunt Nelida put down her book.

"Isabella, it is almost six. It is time to return home."

I had honestly doubted the woman would last that long. However, she seemed to have had a pleasurable day, too, especially as the girls often included her in discussions, asking questions, and listening intently to the lady's prodigious answers.

"Oh, my goodness!" Concepción cried. "I should have been back long ago to help Aunt Herminia with the evening meal."

"Go on ahead. My scooter is up in the lot. Take it. Josh and I can take the shuttle back," Alejandro said as we hastily began gathering up our stuff.

"You can ride back with us," Isabella said.

"That would be great, if there's room in your car."

"Papa's limo has loads of room."

As we left the beach and walked to the waiting limo, Alejandro noticed two men sitting on the deck of a café. Running up to them, he said something, and then returned. I recognized them as the guys from Italy.

"That's their yacht out there," Alejandro said, nodding toward a large, white, three-deck boat. "I just reminded them about dinner. They'll be along shortly."

I thought it odd that both were dressed in slacks

and white shirts, the same as when we bumped into one another on the street last evening. Already well-tanned, I guessed they were just enjoying the cool, ocean breeze without getting toasted like the rest of us, and thought no more of it. Obviously not desirous of missing one of Aunt Herminia's meals, they weren't too far behind as her chauffeur took us back to town.

"Are you staying at the de la Vasquez villa?" Isabella asked Josh.

"No. I have a room above the African Treasures jewelry shop."

Alejandro gave him a peculiar look. "How did you come to stay there?"

"I met its owner, Rami Rasheed, on the Internet several years ago, and then in person in Paris last summer at a festival. Knowing my interests in archaeology, he told me about the treasure you discovered and offered a place to stay when I came."

"Oh." I could tell something bothered my brother.

"I love that shop. He creates some beautiful things," Isabella said.

"He is a very talented person."

Chapter 6

Shadows

Isabella would have dropped Josh off at the shop's front door except the limo couldn't negotiate the narrow street, but did come within a hundred yards. We then passed through the wide, arched gate entrance of Isabella's villa, stopping at the front door. I felt emboldened. "Would you like to go to the disco tonight?"

"Oh, I cannot. I am not allowed to go there."

"Not even with a chaperon?"

"No. She could not possibly keep an eye on me. Too many people," she whispered. "I really had a wonderful time today. Thank you so very much."

"I hope you weren't let down with all our visitors."

"Oh, no. I hardly ever get to mingle with others

my age. It was wonderful. I would like to do it again."

"I'll ask your mother about this Saturday?"

"Fantastic! This time I will provide the lunch," she bubbled, and then whispered, "See if the others perhaps would join us."

"I think I can arrange something," I replied and kissed her hand under the scrutiny of eagle-eyed Aunt Nelida.

"She's really a nice girl," Alejandro remarked as I rejoined him where my scooter was parked. "Super body. Too bad about that nose."

"Physical qualities are not always important."

"Yes, I know, but it helps," Alejandro responded. "She does have nice eyes."

With Alejandro riding on the back, I drove through town having to stop frequently for pedestrians. I was feeling very good about the whole turn of events until that ticklish feeling resonated along my spine, the one I should pay attention to. A couple of my brother's soccer mates called out a greeting and we stopped to chat for a moment. I used the opportunity and casually looked around. People were scattered along the street in the two blocks I could see. A few cars were parked at the curb by a food store or in the process of snaking through the pedestrians using the whole of the street as a sidewalk. Nothing seemed out of place, so with a shrug, convinced myself the feeling was just from being tired. Still, the sensation was not easily shaken. Paranoia settled in to keep me alert.

Several times I noticed people taking pictures,

but only one may have been pointing the thing at me. He did look suspiciously like paparazzi although well-disguised in a Hawaiian shirt, brightly flowered shorts, and flip-flops. I liked his choice of shorts, but this cool slap in the face by paranoia got my attention so decided to give the sporadic warnings some thought – after dinner.

Following a quick shower to send any residual sand back where it belonged, a very satisfying day was topped off with an equally satisfying meal. Full and tired, I kicked off my sandals and spread out on a second story lounger facing a great view of mountains rolling off to the west. As a gentle breeze sung its sweet melody through some windchimes, my mind drift along with the sprinkle of popcorn clouds, contemplating the warning. Later that evening Alejandro shook my shoulder.

"Are you going dancing tonight?" he asked.

"Think I'll pass. I'm pretty used up. Maybe enough energy to make it up to bed and that's it."

He dropped into the lounge next to me. "Me, too." We just quietly sat gazing at the stars.

"What? No disco tonight?" Sis asked somewhat later. "Well, Josh and I are heading there. See you later."

Everyone was startled when we took to our rooms. It was before midnight. I didn't say anything about the vision that had come while half asleep on the lounger, nor the replay during the night. It was so convoluted and distorted to be meaningless – a fishing boat on the ocean, racing along a dirt road with Alejandro behind the wheel of a vehicle (that was scary enough in itself), and a whole army of guys pointing guns at me.

Like the dreams I had about sailing on a tall ship, it seems they have to be repeated numerous times before making sense. So these swatches of premonitions repeated at least three times during the night, but neither clarity nor understanding improved.

For the first time since arriving, I was up with the chickens, even beating Sis to the kitchen. That afforded another first, seeing her before the ritual morning make-over. Her unpinned hair cascade in wavy, wild rivulets to her chest, normally effervescent eyes were dull and blurred. The baggy pair of cotton pj's did nothing for her figure, either. Seeing me, her mouth opened to say something, then closed. It was too late to hide.

"Good morning," she mumbled, sounding grumpy.

"Hi," I tossed over my shoulder while helping Aunt Herminia prepare breakfast for some guests leaving early on a tour to El Gulfo. "You and Josh have a nice time last night?"

Mumbling something about it being fine, she flopped into a chair and crossed her legs, propping her head off the table with one hand to look totally disgusted. I poured some hot chocolate and presented it with a plate of toast.

"Would you like Eggs Benedict?"

"You cooking?"

"Yep. I'm learning."

"Sure," she answered flatly.

While preparing the order I kept glancing over my shoulder until she asked defensively, "So, what are you looking at?"

"Sorry. I've never seen you like that."

"I'm a mess," she snapped and pushed away from the table.

"Maybe, but you're still pretty." Once again, my mouth unhinged out of control.

She stopped half out of the seat and stared, obviously assessing my sincerity. Sitting back down, the dark color in her cheeks darkened. I looked again.

"Now what?"

"Has anyone ever told you how pretty you are when you get mad?"

"What!"

"Your cheeks get kinda dark, and your eyes glow, and your lips sorta pucker, and your nostrils flare a little." My mouth was completely amok.

"And you find that pretty?"

I felt heat saturate my cheeks.

"Has any girl told you how cute you look when you get embarrassed?" she asked, conjuring a faint smile.

"Well, look who we have awake this early," Papa said, breaking in. "So what do we have for breakfast?"

"Eggs Benedict," Concepción announced. "David's cooking."

"Is that safe?" he kidded, heading for the refrigerator to get a glass of milk.

"So, what are your plans for today? Going to

the beach with Señorita Calderõn again?" Sis asked, feeling more herself.

"No. Not until this weekend."

"O-o-h. Barely home and twice in one week."

"She's a nice girl."

"Who?" Alejandro asked midst a cavernous yawn as he padded barefoot into the kitchen.

"Isabella. David has another date with her this weekend."

"I know. She's a nice girl."

"Oh, no. Not you, too?"

"What?"

"Her weird self just woke up. I'm going up to take a shower. Keep an eye on her."

I was absolutely positive one or both would bite on that worm. One thing I got changed the day before was the shower head, from one fixed to the wall to one on a hose, so that when, not if, the hot water suddenly disappeared the stream could be quickly pointed away. When I came down looking as refreshed as I felt, and having heard no scream, the two were beside themselves. "Why didn't it work?" was engraved all over their guilty faces.

"You're gonna have to get up a lot earlier than the average bear." My imitation of Yogi Bear has always been pretty good. "Better luck next time. I'm going shopping."

Timing couldn't have been better. Bathrooms are in pairs, one for women and one for guys. One pair next to the second floor family rooms was just for us, Concepción in one, Alejandro in the other, and me in the lower level utility room, having secretly doubled back to fiddle with the hot water flow. I rather thought the two shrieks harmonized quite well. Cousin Bennie knowingly clued me in as how the system worked. You gotta love relatives with a similar sense of humor.

It was a little early for most of the teens I knew to be wandering about, but I was window shopping anyway. Cutting through a narrow alley passed off as a street, that creepy feeling suddenly chilled my backbone so strong the base of my head ached. *"Run!"* a voice said. But why? After last year, I questioned the feeling only after shifting my legs into high gear. Although in good physical shape, upon reaching the end of the alley and swallowed up in a crowd, I was winded as if just finishing a marathon. Looking back down the long alley, I thought to see movement in the distant shadows.

"Hi, David. Oh, I am sorry. Did I startle you?"

"Ah-h, kinda. I had my mind on something. How are you this morning, Kessare?"

"Very well. Was the swim suit satisfactory?"

"Oh, yeah. It was fine," I mumbled, glancing down the alley once more, but saw nothing and passed off the incident as an over-active, paranoiac imagination. "I felt exposed in that thing at first, but over-dressed after looking around."

She laughed. "I am sorry we gave you such a bad time in the shop."

"I expect it from Sis. Wouldn't be worth getting up knowing she wasn't planning something . . . fun."

"I am going to stop at Cayo's for coffee. Do you

have time to join me?"

"Sure. I'd like to ask you about finding a gift anyway," I answered, looking over her shoulder toward the alley one last time. Josh stepped out of the shadowy depths of the alley and looked around before walking off the opposite direction.

"For a girl?" she said, wiggling her left eyebrow and smiling.

My blush was answer enough as I continued to wonder about the warning. Was there a connection between it and Josh?

Chapter 7

Birds and Bees

The Cayo family has operated a café in Valverde for at least thirteen generations, a picture-book sort of hangout mostly for older folk, thirty and over. Located in the same spot, only the shape changed as the main structure was enlarged to accommodate each proprietors' burgeoning family. A cream-colored, stuccoed building with dark red trim, it is set back from the street to accommodate a large patio surrounded by a wrought iron railing along the front and two sides. It is here the more settled masses huddle around tiny, iron tables barely large enough to hold a coffee cup beneath brightly striped umbrellas in variations of blue or yellow with white. Just in case no one catches the connection, the proprietor has the Canary Island flag prominently displayed from a second story balcony.

Señor Cayo is a plump ball of joviality bouncing from one table to another, never missing a customer or the opportunity to turn an extra sale. Like just about everyone on El Hierro, he is relation, a real one to me, an Evreux on the maternal line more times removed than I can count. With a substantial income from the increased tourist trade, he lives comfortably with his wife and nine children in rooms above. If anyone in the community falls on hard times, Señor Cayo is the first to hear about it and the first to help. His heart is as big as his belly. Maybe that's why his white apron strains so, to keep his shirt buttons from popping off and hold all that love in to be shared evenly.

"My cousin does me honor today," he bubbled while offering up a steaming cup of midnight black coffee to Kessare, and me a rich, smooth hot chocolate along with a couple cakes. "You put your money away, Don David. It is no good here," he said with a fake scowl. "Without you I would be a poor man. I should pay you to come here."

"You were never a poor man, Cousin Cayo. Even if you didn't have a peseta you would be wealthy beyond my meager bank account."

"Oh, really, and how so, you with a bank account in nine numbers or is it ten?"

"There are things far more valuable in the world than money – a good wife, beautiful children, family, and God."

Flabbergasted, he stared at me for a moment

before leaning over to kiss my forehead. Turning to wipe a tear from his puffy eyes, he lumbered away to disappear inside.

"Why David, that was beautiful," Kessare said softly.

Stemming from an impulsive bent, my often-errant lips were want to say the wrong thing. Dodging that bullet it is important to say the right thing, and I have to credit the Captain with helping me in the past; however, those words to Cousin Cayo were the thoughts of my heart. They truly expressed things that began to solidify over the past year thanks to some of the captain's writings.

"So, you felt uncomfortable at the beach in your new swim suit?" she said, getting back to our original conversation.

"Yeah. I mean, geez! At first I felt almost naked. But I got over that when I saw everyone else wearing bikinis . . . or less."

Her laugh was a song capable of raising the most down-hearted person. "That is good. You are what they say, a little Victorian. I chose that suit especially. It is conservative enough for your personality, yet allows you to advertise."

"Huh?"

"Oh, David, look at these flowers?" she said, indicating a vase of fresh-cut posies on the table. "They are brightly colored and give off wonderful smells for what reason? To attract birds, or bees, or insects to help them pollinate and thus reproduce."

"I kinda know about the birds and the bees, Kessare," I replied, trying to hide my embarrassment by taking a sip of chocolate.

"You have been to bed with a girl!"

I choked, spitting chocolate back into the cup. "No!"

"Then let me tell you how it works getting there."

My brain frantically began whipping down every available corridor to find a way to sidetrack this conversation. It obviously was so shell-shocked the thing went into overload and blanked out like a dead computer screen.

"Girls want to attract the attention of boys," she continued, "So they make their hair just so, and apply makeup to cover the tiniest blemish to look pretty. Then they apply just the right fragrance to make a boy's nose twitch in case he isn't already looking. They will spend hours doing this."

"I know. Concepción spends hours in the bathroom."

"Exactly, because she is trying to impress a boy."

"She is? Who?"

"That's not important, but the day shall come he will know. However, once a girl has done all that is possible she will search and search through her wardrobe to find just the right thing to wear. Clothes are important. They make a statement about that person, but how they are worn is even more important.

"For instance, when a girl goes to the disco she wants to attract the attention of boys, of course. It is no fun to sit at a table alone or with other girls.

So, she wears a blouse with the collar open. It must be open just enough to display her crucifix so everyone knows she is a good Catholic girl, but also open to a point just above her cleavage to get a boy to notice other things. She then ties the tails of her blouse into a knot just below the breastbone to expose her belly, in that way a boy can see her tummy is smooth and flat. She wears form-fitting slacks to show the swell of her hips and firm butt."

I coughed. This was way more than I wanted to know.

"The pant leg is tight to show the length and curve of her legs," she continued. "All of this is to attract the attention of boys and tickle their imagination. She hopes they will be like bees and swarm about so she can choose which one she likes best.

"Now boys! What do they do? They do not spend nearly as much time in the bathroom, perhaps only an hour, taking long showers to cool their blood, combing their hair until it is just so, and putting on just the right fragrance girls will like. They leave their shirt unbuttoned to show off their manly chest, and tight trousers so that a bulge shows in their crotch."

With a firm grip on the cup, I held it in front of my mouth to camouflaged the fact that the appendage was unhinged from shock. Her description was painfully blunt – and accurate. Alejandro and I were hands down guilty of exactly what she was saying, although he had backed off from the extreme embraced last year. I began to wonder if Concepción had a hand in this lecture.

"I have known boys to pad their crotch to appear more manly. Oh, it is nothing more than some girls do to their bras. But, on the beach, well, that is different. Nothing can be hidden with beach fashion, unless you are far to the north where beachwear includes a heavy coat. Here, everything is on display and people flaunt everything they have. Boys are said to be the aggressors, but do not be fooled, David. Girls can be very aggressive, too.

"On the beach, for instance, girls wear just enough to cover themselves to remain modest, yet lure a boy's eyes in their direction. So do the boys. Your swim suite is not very revealing compared to the thong Concepción teased you with, and that was relatively modest compared to some things I have seen. On some beaches along the Mediterranean, they wear nothing at all, but that takes away all the teasing and sense of wonder, and spoils everything. Here, you still wonder, think, and dream, which makes the game more exciting.

"Now, the girls spread their beach towels and oil their bodies while watching the boys play their games of volleyball, soccer, or Frisbee, whatever, carefully evaluating each one, secretly dreaming how it would be to have certain ones come and sit by them. Just to be sure they are noticed, they will walk out to the water, but never over ankle deep. She is a flower waiving in the breeze saying 'Yoo-hoo, hello, over here.'

"Of course, the boys are not so innocent. They walk the beach and find the places where attractive girls have set up and then play their games in just the right places so the girls can see them. Eventually, a ball or Frisbee will go astray and land near the girl. They come to get it and apologize. This is to see close up if the girl is something worth further attention. If not, he returns to the game and perhaps moves toward another gathering of flowers. If she is someone who stirs interest, he strikes up a conversation and stays."

I continued to stare at Kessare in utter shock at this impromptu lesson, my gapping mouth partially hidden behind the cup, head tilted slightly to one side, eyes unblinking. I couldn't believe what she was saying. It was true. I'd seen it, but never gave it any thought. How naive! I'd been doing it myself! Now I began to understand why people continue to use that ridiculous simile about the birds and the bees. The game was all about getting a mate, climbing into bed, and assuring another crop of the species. Kessare was just filling in the fine points of how it comes together.

Clearing my throat, I was finally able to speak. "Is that how you got your husband?"

Kessare's face turned a delicate pink as her red lips turned upward at the corners.

"Yes, but what I have told you is only the introduction, David. Just because the bee comes to check out the flower does not mean it is the right bee. Something else must happen, within your breast. Physically, a person can be very stimulating, but how does she make you feel here, inside?" She laid the palm of her hand upon her chest. "Too many times a boy and girl do not take that moment to consider such things. They jump into bed and make love and that is all that matters. Later, they discover something is wrong with the relationship. Cuddling is fun, but there must be something more or the next pretty flower that comes along lures the mate away, or when the body becomes too wrinkled and tired for such play, life becomes endless days of hollowness."

"Did you have sex with your husband before getting married?" Well, there went my mouth again. "I'm sorry. That's none of my business." The way my face felt, it was in flames.

Again Kessare blushed, a little more this time. "Yes. We were pretty young. He was seventeen. I was sixteen. We had known each other forever. Growing up in a place like Valverde everyone knows everyone else. However, each of our parents set us down and told us these things, and what can be called "the day after." We dated a long time. Nearly two years. We knew each was meant for the other so began living together as husband and wife. He is such a wonderful man. We were married in the church just after this past Christmas."

"So where is he? I haven't seen him around."

"He is attending school in Barcelona. He is becoming a chef. He will be home in a few weeks. You must meet him. You two are very much alike. That is why I am telling you this. It is best to know what you are doing and how to go about it properly. Oh, do not worry so much about the flirting, shopping, and sorting. Just be aware of your feelings, the real ones, in your heart, before selecting the merchandise. A great piece of advice came from Señor Cayo when my Ramon and I were having a cup of coffee a few days before our wedding. He came over and whispered, "Remember, all sales are final. No returns.""

As we separated, my head was like a pot of water in a rolling boil from all this sudden revelation. I waived to Cousin Cayo, and then spotted the two Italian men who were staying at the villa. They were seated at the far end of the patio sipping coffee. One was talking with cousin's oldest daughter. The one not occupied smiled and waved back. They seemed to be leaving as well. Then I remembered what I had wanted to ask Kessare and ran after her.

"What gift do you suggest for a girl who has everything?"

"And who would that be? Concepción?"

"No." I faltered then answered, "Isabella Calderõn."

"Hum-m, let me see. Yes. There is a place right down the street that might have something."

The African Treasures is a long shop barely wide enough for three people to stand touching outstretched fingertips. Its proprietor, Rami Rasheed, sat hunched over a small, heavy, wood table using a small torch to weld wire.

"I will be with you in a moment, please," he said, continuing to work on something secured in a miniature clamp. Seconds later, he turned off the torch. "I apologize most sincerely, but . . ."

"We completely understand," Kessare said. "Delicate workmanship must not be interrupted until completed."

Spotting me, Rami's eyes became large, white pools with a dark island floating in the middle as a large smile stretched across his dark, brown face. Reaching out long, slender fingers, he shook my hand. "*Assalamu alaikum*, Peace be upon you," he said, his voice clear and firm.

"Peace be upon you," I replied, not about to attempt to speak Arabic just yet, although the Captain detailed some of the language and customs in his journal.

"My place is honored by your presence, Don David. How may I help you?"

"Don David . . .," Kessare began, but I interrupted.

"Just David, please."

"David is looking for a special gift for a friend."

"For a man or woman?"

"A woman. A daughter of Spain," Kessare said.

"Señorita Isabella Calderõn, to be specific," I said.

"Ah-h-h, Señorita Calderõn. She frequents this establishment often. She was here just the other day with her chaperone looking at hair combs."

I would have purchased the expensive one first presented, but Kessare guided me to something more modest in price, yet very beautiful. She was right. Everyone knew everyone else in Valverde and Kessare was in the front ranks. Her suggestion was perfect for Isabella's hair color. As Rami wrapped it in beautiful paper, I added a note.

Hi, Isabella.
I saw this in a shop and immediately thought it perfect for your hair.
Thank you for a wonderful time at the beach.
David

Of course, Kessare helped me with the wording. Typically my penmanship isn't all that great, and my hand shook enough to make it unreadable. After messing up the first two note cards, I asked Kessare to write it, but she insisted such a message should be in my hand.

"I assume you accept that scrawling as proficient penmanship?" the captain commented on my sloppy handwriting as he hovered over my shoulder during some early dictation about his career. "You should work on it."

"What's to work on? Everything is done on computers these days. Doing it this way is nuts."

"Not everything, Francis. Someday it might be important. Work on it."

Of course I did. It improved and actually took on a very nice appearance . . . when slowing down. However, my mind works far too fast, faster than I can type at times, and at over sixty words per minute, clocked, that's pretty fast. Slowing way down, the third attempt at Isabella's note was better, at least legible. Hands still shaking, I delivered the gift to her villa personally.

"Would Don Evreux wish to come inside and present this to the Señorita himself?" their *sirviente* asked.

"No, sir. I can't stay. Got another appointment. I just wanted to make sure this was delivered today. Thank you," I more or less babbled and took off. Why? That was the perfect excuse to see her again and I blew it!

That evening, as we dined on the family patio overlooking the flower garden outside of the kitchen, the Calderõn chauffeur came through the kitchen and approached the table. A tall, lean, ramrod in a form-fitting suit, cap and gloves, the guy in his late twenties reminded me of a bullfighter in silver-gray. Rising to greet him, he handed me an envelope, executed a slight bow, and left. Fingers shaking, I tried to pry it open while looking cool.

"I can smell the perfume from here," Sis snickered. "It's from Isabella."

"Geez! And her family chauffeur wasn't a clue?" I answered with more than a hint of dripping sarcasm. Looking up, all eyes were on me. "Just a thank you, ah, for the outing."

"And perhaps that little gift?"

"Concepción, you are far too nosey," I snapped and sat down in a funk, stuffing the letter in my shirt pocket so to smell the light, violet fragrance, and finish dinner.

That evening, while preparing for the disco, I seemed more deliberate or at least more conscious of what was going on. A shower, a liberal sprinkle of toilet water, a new pair of trousers of stretch material so they clung like a second skin to my hips, butt and thighs. Pant legs were shoved into the boots now polished to a mirror gloss. I thought about tying my shirt into a knot in front to show off my burgeoning six-pack, but considered that might be a bit girlish. Still, it was something to be proud of considering how a lot of guys in my school back in Lincoln tended to soft and flabby. I left the shirt unbuttoned nearly to the naval to display the gold chain with the old, iron key dangling against my hairless chest.

Sis was right about the hair conditioner. Lubricating usually unmanageable locks made them more easily brushed. She was more than happy to braid it into the double-tied pony tail low on the nape. The old-fashioned look was distinctive and complementary. A bright blue headband with the ends hanging down the back matched the one around my waist. Standing in the mirror I had to admit to looking very dashing. I certainly didn't need any padding. The mascara snitched from Sis darkened the growth of hair over my upper lip perfectly so it stood out against my dark skin.

"Hey, Zorro!" I said to the mirror.

Hey, Zorro," Alejandro echoed, coming into the room. "Looking good, brother."

He was a lot more conservatively attired. Over the last year our dress styles completely flip-flopped. His shirt was only unbutton two from the top and the trousers were looser.

For the first time in my life, the closer I came to the disco house the more relaxed I felt, hitting the dance floor soon after passing through the crowded entrance. I now understood the game and was anxious to test out the rules. Of course, with that many active kids the temp got pretty warm and I began sweating like a pig. The remedy was to drink lots of juice and occasionally step outside to catch some of the almost constant breeze. What surprised me was waking up in bed the next morning without knowing how I came to be there. Swinging leaden legs off the edge of the bed I clutched my head as a bass drum banged away inside that wouldn't stop. I fell back holding it before the thing exploded.

"Well, good morning Casanova," Concepción said, coming into the room and opening the curtains. The sudden flood of light sent me diving beneath the covers with a massive groan.

"What happened?"

"At what particular point in time?"

"How'd I get here?"

"Alejandro and Josh carried you back after you passed out."

"Too much excitement, I guess."

"Too much vino, I guess," she said, sounding really sour.

"I didn't touch any of that stuff. Oh, geez! It feels like I've been hit with a hatchet."

"Serves you right," she hammered and stomped out.

When the hatchet attack subsided some, I peeked out from under the covers to see Alejandro's bare feet shuffle through the door. He was still in pajamas.

"How are you feeling?"

"Terrible. What happened?"

"At what point in time?"

"Concepción asked that already. What are you guys talking about?"

"Well, first you became the dance king, and then started acting very strange. You latched onto this one chick, an off-islander. Have to hand it to you, you know how to pick the hot ones. You curled up in a dark corner and had your hands all over her then go out back to cool off. Yeah, cool off. She was all over you with her lips. I think you were actually about to have sex right there when Sis came along. When she said something, you got really mad. You said some mean things. I heard you, brother. She slapped your face. You deserved it. You were lucky it was only a slap. You were so drunk you could not walk. She was very hurt and left. You fell and could not stand up so Josh and I carried you back here and put you in bed."

"What do you mean I was drunk. All I ever drink there is fruit juice."

"You were drunk, brother. Drunk on your butt." Alejandro was upset.

"I didn't . . . ." I began to protest, but the pain in my head on a scale of one to ten shot to eleven as I grabbed the two sides in an attempt to hold them together.

When I awoke sometime later, Concepción was sponging my forehead with a cool towel. The pain was less, despite a persistent echo.

"Hello," she said, still sounding cool.

"Hi," I answered, my mouth feeling as if filled with more sand than on the beach.

"Feeling better?"

"A little."

"You shouldn't drink so much."

"Concepción?"

"What?"

"I'm sorry."

"It was the alcohol."

"I . . ."

She looked at me with those puppy brown eyes. There was hurt there.

"I swear, I never touched any alcohol."

"You certainly acted like it."

"Honest. I'd never lie to you."

She patted the beads of perspiration on my forehead with the towel again.

Slowly rising to sit on the edge of the bed I said, "I don't know what I said. You're like a sister. I love you too much to hurt you. Whatever happened, I'm sorry. Really."

She took both my hands into her's and stared into my eyes. "Alejandro had a dog since he was born. It watched him better than any babysitter. It was the most gentle creature. Then one day, when our brother was eight, he found his dog having sex with another dog. He thought it would be fun to break it up. His dog became angry and bit him. That's where the scar on his left forearm came from. Anyway, the dog was terribly upset it had hurt Alejandro. When they returned home from the doctor it came to Alejandro, tail between its legs, its head bowed, and whined. It knew it had done wrong and was sorry. Alejandro knew he had provoked the incident. It was forgotten. They continued to be friends." She bent over and kissed my cheek.

"Thank you," I replied, feeling on the verge of crying, then said, "Alejandro left before I could thank him for carrying me home. He was kinda mad."

"He is upset. They just tossed you on the bed and left."

"But," I replied, silently referring to the fact I was wearing my PJ bottoms.

"I couldn't just let you lay there."

"You . . .?"

"Yes."

I felt the heat rise in my face.

"Your underwear covers more than the swim suit. Feel like eating something?"

"A little. Maybe food will kick this headache," I replied, slowly standing, this time sans the hatchet attack, but felt it lurking close. "What time is it?"

"Eleven."

"Let me take a shower and I'll meet you in the kitchen."

The warm water pouring over my head and body helped calm the pounding and swept away the lethargy. Padding back to my room wrapped in a towel I met Alejandro. He was still stand-offish.

"I came to apologize," he said.

"You apologize? For what?"

"I treated you badly. I should have helped put you to bed. You were not well."

"Brother, I am totally confused. I honestly don't

remember anything after we got to the disco. I understand I acted like a donkey. It is me that is sorry."

Pulling on a pair of Bermudas and tee, being careful the way I moved to avoid the onset of another headache he said, "You started acting very strange after meeting that off-islander."

"I don't even remember her. Well, I vaguely remember meeting a kinda short girl, but . . ."

"And built like the cathedral Santa María La Almudena."

"I really don't remember."

We walked down to the kitchen where Concepción had prepared chicken soup and sandwiches. She posed a question that sent a chill down my back.

"Could someone have slipped a drug in one of your drinks?"

"How? Who?"

"Well, that girl you were almost in bed with could have slipped something in one of your drinks."

"But why?"

She rolled her eyes upward. "I warned Alejandro last year about dressing like that, and then you do it. Some girls get very excited by such behavior."

A forest fire rushed to my cheeks. If Smokey Bear were around he would have hit me over the head with his shovel because I was guilty of sparking the problem. Maybe he did, the way it hurt.

"Hello," Josh said as he entered the kitchen.

"How do you feel?"

"A little better."

"We think someone may have drugged him. That *putana.*"

"Alejandro!" Sis snapped.

"After we put you to bed, I started thinking. There were some things about your situation I heard happening at a university near London. So, I returned to the disco and talked to some of the people still there, especially the owner. I mentioned how you got smashed. He was surprised because you only drank bottled fruit drinks."

"See," I emphasized my innocence.

"But what could make David act like he was drunk?" Alejandro asked.

"Rohypnol, for one," Josh answered matter-of-factly.

"What is that?" Concepción asked.

"A very potent hypnotic. In the papers, it is referred to as the date rape drug."

"What!" I yelled and then grabbed my head. It was splitting apart again. Concepción jumped to my shoulders and began massaging them to relieve the pain. "I don't use that crap." The pain had me on the verge of tears.

"From what a couple people said, that girl you were with could have put some in your drink. It is odorless, tasteless, and dissolves rapidly. They said she bought two drinks and stopped briefly to chat with someone before returning to your table. Not long after that you started acting strangely."

"I vaguely remember that. She said it was a

friend and was just saying hello. But, why would she do something like that?" I asked.

"You are naive," Concepción said, rolling her eyes. "Perhaps to get you into bed? You are very wealthy."

"Yeah," Alejandro added, "Get into your trousers and then into your bank account."

With that declaration, the chill tickling my spine rose up into a tidal wave coursing along the spine as now my whole body shivered. "Oh, man!" I groaned, slumping forward into my hands, shivering.

"Something else. Those two from the yacht that have been staying here, they were in the alley with you and the girl. Alejandro came to speak to you about what you said to Concepción, but you turned and collapsed into his arms. They said they would bring you back, but Alejandro threw you over his shoulder and we left." Josh said.

"Do you think they . . .? Oh, that's just paranoid. I need some fresh air," I said. "I'm going for a walk." My friends came along like a Roman phalanx.

Chapter 8

Deja vu

An irritating similarity between Aunt Florence and Grandma was the philosophy, "He who cooks does not do dishes." So, that next morning as Concepción and Josh left to sit together on the patio, Alejandro and I swept the dirtied dishes into the sink and cleaned up before adjourning to our rooms to put on swim suits under travel clothes. While Josh headed for the museum, we three gassed up the scooters and headed to the hacienda, parking in the circular drive out front.

Among the many things done to restore Casa de St. Nazaire was a project my brother and sister undertook – clearing the trail down to Dolphin cove. No more battling tangled overgrowth or dodging rocks like a Denver Bronco running back; it was a delightful walk through the pines. The hot pool was something not to be bypassed. I quickly tossed off my clothes and jumped in wearing the bikini from the other day, feeling less self-conscious, especially in company of family. Reaching the middle of the man-made pond I turned to look back.

Alejandro recklessly dove in with a belly flop, but my gaze settled on Sis. Again clad in a two-piece swimsuit she carefully negotiated the slippery rocks until submerged to her long neck. A tingling feeling tickled the area between my shoulder blades up to the base of my head, the danger warning. Not understanding that signal last year resulted in Alejandro being tortured and the resultant scars. I may have had the warning the other night, but don't remember, not that I wanted to remember that nightmare. In any event, whenever I failed to heed it something unpleasant happened. I was confused. What danger could be lurking here in this lonely piece of paradise?

The usual horseplay was absent as we each seemed to be introspective. That was God-sent. I needed some time to sort things out.

Over the past year, some girls had caused me to become nervous and sweaty. While having moved to overcome a long, debilitating shyness, I was far from becoming aggressive. Learning of my disgusting behavior last night furthered a depression that had been settling over me as we neared Casa St. Nazaire. We were all convinced the incident had been drug-induced, but I couldn't accept that as an excuse. I thought of how I had looked at Isabella and Concepción at the beach and the accompanying sensations. If drugs could knock down the barrier restraining cave man instincts, I had to be super careful, even with alcohol. I shivered to think I could be a Jekyll and Hyde with only a chemical potion separating two personalities.

Then my mind settled on Kessare's lecture. It had been a warning. I ignored the wisdom and mis-used that knowledge. Next came a remembrance of those sex ed classes in school. We guys oogled the drawings, fantasied, and cracked adolescent jokes. Mr. Goeglien was patient with our immature behav-ior, but his warning now sounded very loud and clear.

"Very soon those male hormones sleeping in your bodies will wake up. Then you will be singing a different tune. They have a great power. If you aren't careful they will possess your body as if al-iens, turning you into something you won't like, and cause a lot of pain."

We laughed, then. I wasn't laughing now.

A sudden wall of water splashed over me. Clear-ing my eyes, it had come from Concepción resulting in twenty minutes of light-hearted splashing and runs under the cold waterfall before beaching to talk and dry. A couple times my body quivered involun-tarily. I tried not to look at Concepción's smooth, brown body. When a spasm reverberated up my spine one more time I jumped up with a "let's go," and quickly dressed. Minutes later we walked out to the end of the dragon's head, but the tingling wouldn't go away. When a white yacht hove around the opposite point into the cove, I realized I had obviously misinterpreted the warning – again. Alejandro and Concepción followed as I instantly flattened on the ground to watch.

"Girls!" I snorted to myself. "When will I ever understand!"

"That's the boat those Italians arrived on. What's it doing here?" Alejandro asked.

"Beats me. I don't think they know we're here. Let's just watch," the tingling got stronger as a cold chill now did an Iditarod up and down my back not unlike the other day in the alley, only stronger. I knew we should take flight.

"Let's get out of here," I said.

"Wait a moment. We're okay. They can't see us," Alejandro said. Why we whispered at the time beat me.

The boat dropped anchor the length of a football field off shore. Presently, a rubberized, motor launch carried four men to the beach. Two of them walked up to where the cabin was being rebuilt. They were just returning when I heard the Captain's voice.

"Behind you, Francis."

The two Italians from Aunt Herminia's villa were coming toward us. I didn't need any prompting to realize we were in trouble. All three of us stood slowly and faced them as they approached to within a hundred feeet. When they reached inside their sport jackets and pulled out pistols there was no hesitation. With a unified move, we bailed off the edge.

The launch was pulling away from shore about the time we hit the water. The hope was to make the needle's eye and hide in the cave, but it would be close. We had reached the far side of the eye when three in the boat climbed ashore. A fourth piloted around the end of the volcanic arm. We ran for all we were worth. That they meant us harm became obvious when a bullet ricochet off the cliff face ahead of us. That only lent speed to our feet. The rocks were slippery, but our shoes clung fast while theirs slipped causing them a lot of difficulty and more errant shots. Ducking through the waterfall, I knew we couldn't go very far because of the dark, with no time to strike a torch. But, we could go far enough to put Alejandro's plan to work.

Leaving the trail, we silently slipped into the water channel and ducked beneath an overhang. Above we heard their footsteps and heavy breathing as the three ran past and deeper into the cave. They had a flashlight. Then the launch entered the cave. The pilot had one, too. Taking a deep breathe we slipped below the surface and watched as he drift pass before surfacing.

"What will we do?" Concepción whispered when we surfaced.

"Let's swim out and hide among the rocks," I suggested.

We were able to move some distance from the entrance, but our predicament wasn't greatly improved. It was almost six miles south along the rugged coastline to an area where the cliff could be negotiated back to the top. The other choice was to wait them out, hoping they would give up and leave. After an hour it became evident that wasn't going to happen and our secret position becoming less tenable.

Reluctantly, we started swimming south trying to keep from being seen and from being tossed into the rocky coastline. The surf was much heavier away from our protected cove. That's when a fin appeared next to each of us. Latching on, I prayed they wouldn't take us back, but no, our friends carried us safely south along the coast, mile after mile. Now I truly understood how it must have been for my ancestor when they first brought him to El Hierro.

Arriving at a minuscule beach at the base of a defile, we collapsed on the black volcanic sand. The dolphins could have taken us on to the village two miles further south and wondered why they hadn't. Tired and still feeling the effects of the previous night, I closed my eyes for a moment. It was Concepción poking me in the ribs that brought me back to reality. It was nearly dark.

"I must have fallen asleep," I said.

"You have had a rough vacation, so we let you rest," Alejandro said.

"We'll have to stay here," Sis said.

That was obvious. Climbing the fissure to the top would be tricky in daylight. Finding a comfortable spot was not going to be easy, either. High tide threatened to devour much of the beach, and the waves were beginning to nibble away at it. Morning found us huddled closely together as it had turned cool. Bodies sore and tired from the ordeal stiffened to the consistency of cardboard. The first glint of sunlight felt like a cup of hot chocolate on a Nebraska winter morning, but that presented another fear. If those men came looking in this direction they would surely see us climbing the cliff. Still, we had no choice. When we thought to try swimming to the village, the dolphins blocked our way, a clear indication that wasn't a good idea. Clouds on the horizon indicated a squall meaning increased surf that would push us into the rocky coastline.

Much of the morning was spent reaching the top, constantly glancing over our shoulders expecting to see the launch or yacht hove into view. On that score we were fortunate. Thankfully, we had presence of mind to tie our tennis shoes around our necks instead of jettisoning them at first flight. Negotiating the sharp, volcanic rock would have been impossible in bare feet. As it was, our shoes became shredded and feet still took a beating.

The climb itself wasn't technical, just steep, shielding us for the most part from the ocean, but once on top we collapsed and slept several hours. I was the first to be aroused thanks to one of the giant lizards sniffing my feet, it's pink tongue flipping in and out. You really don't know what it's like waking up to be greeted by one of those docile creatures the size of large hog. Once the heart stops palpitating, it is possible to become oriented and get on with – in this case – survival.

"I don't think we can return to the hacienda from here without becoming lost," Alejandro admitted. "The village is not far. It should not be too difficult getting there and much easier to pick up the trail north to the hacienda. If they have a telephone or radio we might be able to call papa."

I think Sis was surprised her brother didn't forge ahead and get us lost. She often chided him with, "Just like a man, never ask directions," but our adventurous spirit was thoroughly doused by the watery escape, overnight camp out, and climb. My feet hurt and was sure theirs did, too. Instead, Alejandro's suggestion was only sound logic. And we could get something to eat at the village, too.

His estimation of the distance to the village was pretty accurate, and we made good time thanks to what must have been an animal trail. However, as we crested a knoll overlooking the village clustered near the beach a quarter mile distant, Concepción suddenly stopped and dropped to a crouch.

"Get down!" she whispered as if anyone down there would hear. "Look! On the beach."

Squinting to check out what had excited her, my heart sank. It was the rubber launch.

"They're in the village. Probably looking for us."

"Well, so much for getting something to eat. That's the trail back to the hacienda," Alejandro moaned, pointing to a thin line winding up the volcanic slope from the village. "We can pick it up by going west from here."

Once surmounting the ragged rocks plunging into the sea, the top terrain becomes rolling grasslands and barren, volcanic domes. It's easily negotiated, but leaves one feeling awfully exposed. Keeping to tree groves at least helped alleviate that fear.

Another problem was that Alejandro's comment was right about food. None of us had eaten since yesterday's noontime breakfast. At least we found fresh water in rocky pockets.

"How about lizard?" I suggested as my stomach put up an audible howl.

"I'd rather eat shoe leather. Besides, how do you plan to kill it and get through that tough hide?"

"At this point, I'll use my teeth."

"Well, Enjoy. I will wait until getting back to the hacienda," Sis replied.

"Ah, guys? What if they're taking this trail back, too?"

"We will deal with that if it presents itself. Right now I am too tired and hungry to care about what-ifs," Alejandro grumbled.

Less than 20 minutes later we crossed the trail and headed for home. Two hours later we stood on the hill overlooking the plantation from the south. It appeared deserted.

"Where are the scooters?" Sis asked as we hunkered among some trees and rocks watching for any signs of unfriendly life.

"Must have hidden them. When we didn't show up last night papa would look here first. No scooters, he'd move on," I replied.

Carefully easing down the trail closer to the house, Alejandro's hand suddenly came up sharply against my chest. "There, in the bushes next to the house," he whispered, this time for good reason. We were close enough someone could hear us if they were in hiding.

Our scooters had been carefully hidden in the brush on the south rear side of the house, visible only from our elevated position.

"Stay here. I'll go down and check them out," he said. When he returned it was obvious all was not well. "They cut the battery wires. They're useless."

"Okay," Sis spit defiantly. "We can take the trail west toward Gulfo Bay Road. It is a bit longer, but we can be back to Valverde by tomorrow noon if someone doesn't come along and give us a ride."

"Sabinosa would be closer," Alejandro said.

Seeming to be the only sensible choice, we struck out through the trees to meet up with the trail some distance west of the house. That the path followed the stream helped, too. My belly button was grinding on my backbone. Filling with water at least helped alleviate some of the discomfort. When I saw one of the big lizards standing not far off, it looked mighty tasty.

Toward five in the afternoon we found the road. An hour later a car came from Gulfo Bay. Waiving excitedly we jumped for joy. As it slowed to stop Alejandro screamed, "Not that car!" It was the two men from the villa.

There wasn't much cover other than rocks, but we tried to make the most of it especially when gun-shots sent bullets awfully close overhead. That was enough to distract Concepción who stumbled and sprained her ankle. That was it. Hands in the air, we stopped.

Wrists duck taped behind our backs, they drove us to the hacienda to be herded onto the porch to await our fate as another man stepped out chewing on something. A misanthrope hovered in his shadow.

"You have given us quite a chase," he said in broken Spanish. "No matter. Take those two to the cave," he continued with a smug expression, referring to Alejandro and me.

"Can I kill them?" the throwback asked in Italian, giggling through irregular teeth as he twitched nervously. I wasn't sure at the time why we feigned not understanding Italian, but that can sometimes be helpful. My brother and sister understood a little thanks to a language class in school. There was a cute girl at my school whose family emigrated from Italy. She taught me some of her language and I helped her with English so I caught enough of the conversation to know what was going on. If not so dehydrated I might have wet my pants.

"No. You will not kill them," the leader said, narrowing his eyes in anger. "Do as I say. Watch them so they do not escape. Paulo, take the girl to the yacht. Sanchez, round up the others. Felippe, look at your wristwatch. In two hours, we will leave. It takes 20 minutes to go down to the beach. If you are not there in exactly two hours, I will leave you and the authorities will have you. Do you understand?"

"*Si, capo,*" the young man replied, obviously crestfallen.

I guessed the guy giving orders was perhaps in his mid thirties. Nice looking. One would have thought him a banker or insurance salesman, never a gangster. His hair was thick and black, cut short and combed into thin spikes. Like the creature lurking over us, he had heavy eyebrows and straight, narrow nose, but his mouth had a pleasant, deceiving smile. A thin, neatly trimmed mustache over his lip was the same coal black like the hair on his head. A day's growth of beard was black and already heavy.

The crazy one taking charge of us was as hairless as a baby. A heavy crucifix hung around his neck while his boss sported a green, teardrop pendant on a silver chain just below the base of his throat above a thatch of black hair. The boss' voice was low and calm indicative of a man in complete control while psycho had an irritating whine.

Thrown to the dirt floor in the cave, Alejandro and I had our feet bound tightly with more gray-colored duct tape, and a swatch stuck over our mouths. When his confederates disappeared, our guard paced around us like a caged lion, rubbing sweaty hands on his trousers and constantly licking his lips, all the while repeatedly checking at his gold wristwatch.

This character wasn't very tall, perhaps 5-6 and skinny. His coloring was sort of an orangish-tinted brown. Any lack of body hair was certainly made up for top side. Thick, black curls crowded his forehead, over small ears, and wrapped around the base of his small, round skull. Eyebrows arched in a heavy, thick line over and slightly past dark brown eyes. Between them a straight, narrow nose dropped down to overhang a small mouth with thin lips. The jaws were set straight, tapering to a narrow, squared chin, something like the toe on my dancing boots. There was a slight cleavage of the chin. His white, cotton shirt was open to display a heavy, gold chain and part of a tattoo on the left just above the breast, which looked to be a pentagram. It was his eyes, though, that revealed his true nature—narrow, dark, and dilated with excitement as his breath came in short spurts.

Suddenly he stopped, stared at us, a wild glint in those beady eyes. Roughly turned onto my back, he sat on my hips immobilizing movement. Whatever his pea-sized brain had settled on, I was beyond scared. When he produced a long, pearl-covered handle and snapped an equally long blade into position I was petrified.

"Jefe said not to kill. He did not say I could not have a little fun."

The kid was salivating like a starved hyena as he lifted the bottom of my tee-shirt, slipped the blade underneath, and neatly sliced the material until reaching the neckband.

"Oh, careful, do not want to cut pretty throat . . . not just yet."

Just as carefully, he sliced open each sleeve, yanked the material away and gave it a haphazard toss.

When he laid the point of his stiletto at the base of my sternum, I stopped breathing. Then quite unexpectedly, his eyes went wide. Lifting his weight, he stood straddle my ribs. With a soft, sinister snicker, he stepped clear. I tried looking back, but couldn't see who had obviously joined us.

"Does pretty girl think that thing will work?" he asked, stepping clear of my body. That Concepción might have escaped was the only "pretty girl" that came to mind.

"Actually no, but they do work in other ways."

It was Isabella's voice! I desperately struggled to cry out, to warn her about this maniac, but he leaped forward. What followed was a series of weird noises – a grunt as air was forcibly expelled from lungs, and a resounding slap. To my amazement our captor hit the soft dirt floor and plowed several feet face down creating a furrow.

"Oh, I hope we did not kill him," Isabella moaned, stepping into view.

"Umf, umf," I replied through the tape.

Lifting an edge of the tape, she peeled it off with a quick jerk taking a good share of the hair that had been growing on my upper lip.

"Ow!" I wailed.

"What did you say?" she asked seeming lost as what to do next.

"I said, who cares. Quick, untie us."

The next surprise was the appearance of Josh who began freeing Alejandro as Isabella quickly cut my feet free, turned me over, and freed my hands. As I rubbed circulation back into them, Alejandro hollered when he, too, lost most of his lip hair. He had more of it so it really had to have hurt. We'd been pretty proud of that recent development. It might have been faint, but was giving me a truly manly appearance and feel.

Grabbing up the roll of tape left behind, I sat on

the small of maniac's back and glued his hands behind the back, and then tossed the roll to Josh. "Tie
pea-brain's feet. So how'd you guys find us?"

"The whole island is looking for you," Isabella
explained. "Then I received a note a little while ago
saying you needed my help and to come here quickly, but to tell no one. I was to meet Josh at Señor
Cayo's."

"I received a similar note saying much the same
thing, but to meet Señorita Calderõn at the cafe."

"Papa would never allow me to come here alone
with a single man, but we borrowed a scooter from
Señor Cayo and came anyway. There was a man
standing on the porch who said you were here."

"Man? What'd he look like?"

"Oh, a very handsome caballero," she replied.

"At first I thought it was you," Josh said, "Was
that your father?"

"Ah-h, no. That must've been the Captain. He
hangs out here a lot."

"Why didn't he rescue you?" Josh asked.

"It's a long story. We've got an hour to get down
to the boat before they leave," I answered, still a little confused about what the Captain could or could
not do.

"And what do you propose when we get there?
Against all of them with guns?" Alejandro asked.

"I don't know, but I'll think of something.
Thanks, Isabella. You're an angle," I said, giving her a
quick kiss on the cheek. "I want you to go back to
town and get the police. Tell them that Italian gangsters from that fancy yacht that's been in the harbor

have kidnapped Concepción. We're heading to Dolphin Cove to try and stop them. Josh, thanks for your help."

"I do not intend to stand around if Concepción is in danger. Señorita Isabella, can you operate the scooter?" Josh said.

"Oh, yes."

"Then go for help. I am going with David and Alejandro."

I felt a little uncomfortable letting Isabella strike out alone, but there was a side to this girl indicating more beneath that soft, delicate exterior than fluff. Besides, having Josh at our side promoted confidence. We each had studied martial arts and spared a bit on the beach the other day. He was good, and judging by the way the creature in the cave had been neutralized, his skill was more than clubhouse, shadow boxing.

Taking the shortcut along the cold stream, we careened nearly out of control down the steep trail, but as we tumbled onto the plateau next to the cabin, we looked out on the cove in dismay.

"They're gone!" Alejandro vocalized.

"Come on."

"But where, David?" Josh asked.

"That character in the cave will know," I said beginning the ascent.

Now functioning totally on adrenaline, I raced back up the trail, bursting into the cave as a wild man. However, no manner of threats would loosen his tongue.

"Keep an eye on him," I said, disappearing into

the house to rummage through some carpenter's tools. Returning, I was carrying a small sledgehammer and four galvanized pipes, each three-foot long. "The American Indians knew how to get someone to talk," I sort of explained while driving one stake into the ground. "Rip his shirt off."

One outstretched hand taped to the embedded stake, I drove the second a good foot beyond the reach of his other hand. Using more tape, I wrapped it around the wrist, twisted it into rope-shape, put a foot against the stake and pulled until he cried out in pain, and tied it off. When I drove a stake near each foot, Alejandro and Josh grasped the concept seen in American western movies. While Alejandro sat straddle his legs pinning them securely, I none too gently ripped off a shoe and sock, wrapped tape around the ankle, pulled out a length, twisted, and likewise pulling the leg tight. Josh followed my lead with the other foot until our victim was spread-eagled tighter than Papa Montoya's guitar string. Disappearing again into the house, I returned with a plumber's torch and striker.

"I don't think I like what you are planning," Alejandro said.

"The difference between Fuentes and me is that he only wanted treasure. I want Concepción back," I answered.

"The Arabian prophet, Mohammad, said that a woman is the greatest treasure in the world." Josh said.

"Good thought," I answered while energizing the needle-like, blue flame. "Time to reclaim our treasure."

Our captive's eyes went wide as I began heating up the blade of his knife.

"What is he saying?" Alejandro asked as their captive began babbling frantically. Our grasp of Italian was too basic to keep up with the speed he was talking.

"Where are they taking our sister?" I screamed in his face.

"I cannot tell. I am sworn to secrecy," Josh interpreted.

"Wrong answer," I replied and touched the red-hot tip to the bottom of his left foot.

His scream filled the cavern and must have crack some rocks overhead as dust drifted down.

"Where is our sister?" I yelled a second time, but he only answered with an Italian epithet about my family parentage. "Wrong again," I replied and touched the reheated blade to the other foot.

"The side hurts worse," Alejandro said, biting his lower lip.

When creature failed to answer a third time I slowly brought the blade to between the third and fourth rib on his left side. He tried to squirm and pull away. That was useless. When he didn't answer the question, the blade touched him. Before that scream died away, he began crying like a little baby. It didn't take long before he decided these crazed captors would roast him an inch at a time. He spewed information like a shaken soda bottle.

"They will take her to Italy and hold her for ransom."

What we learned was staggering. These guys were Italian Mafia active along the mountainous western coast of southern Italy. Kidnapping children of wealthy, European industrialists and bankers, they held them for ransom. Because of our treasure, we had become a target. They had actually targeted me, but could never find me alone, either in Lincoln or on El Hierro. The decision was then made to take Concepción, reasoning we would be more inclined to pay more, faster.

"His cell phone does not seem to be working," Josh said as he played with the button.

"Probably something in the rock. Alejandro, go outside and call the police and tell them what he said. It's not too late to intercept the boat."

As he dashed out of the cave, the Captain appeared out of the shadows and suggested, "Find out exactly where in Italy they may go, just in case the authorities do not find the boat," and handed Josh some writing paper and pencil from the carpenter's stash.

Despite wondering how anyone could not find that big yacht this close to the island, I didn't question his thinking and put it to my victim. He refused to answer. When Alejandro returned I had the exact destination they would take Sis, and was working on a lot of details, including a list of names. It kept Josh busy interpreting as Alejandro now wrote furiously. When Lt. Carlos arrived, I had a good deal of valuable information.

"Don Evreux, we are a civilized people. We do not torture our prisoners," he admonished.

"One, he wasn't your prisoner. Two, these people are not civilized. Three, I want our sister back, and four I have lost all patience and civility," I retaliated, functioning on pure anger and adrenalin. The last two were as good loosening Jekyll as any drug.

With a gentle smile, Lt. Carlos cupped a big hand behind my head. "We shall get her back." He then stepped outside to relay the information back to Valverde on the radio and have Señor Gonzales' plane in the air to find the boat. He then carefully wrote down everything we recounted of our ordeal before turning to question the guy still staked out. He wasn't being very cooperative, again.

"They tortured me. None of that can be used against me. I am a victim of these crazy children. Untie me."

"Now, now, calm down," Lt. Carlos said as he sat cross-legged next to him. "I think we have a misunderstanding here. Yes, we do. Are you sure those burns are from torture?"

"Yes!" he shrieked, beginning to cry again.

"Well, let me see. Such accusations are serious, very serious, but eventually would come down to your word, a person of questionable character against these young men—both Don Alejandro and also Don David are respected and loved citizens. Some of El Hierro's finest, upstanding citizens. Why, that one is the Marqués de Evreux, patron of our tiny island. And then there is myself, a decorated police officer with many years of stellar service.

"And the judge is my cousin," Alejandro butt in.

"Ah, yes. Judge Bernardo is a very stern man,

and he has a special love for the girl you took. Now, just who do you think the authorities are going to believe?" Carlos asked very casually.

The guy's eyes became wide as chargers. I'd never seen so much white.

"We are a peaceful family on El Hierro, and you have certain rights under our law about confessing. How does that go? I heard it in an American movie and it sounded so professional," Carlos continued using a soothing voice.

"You have the right to remain silent," Josh prompted, obviously an aficionado of American television crime shows.

"Ah, yes. That is it. Thank you, Señor. You have the right to remain silent." He paused and motioned with two fingers over his shoulder for him to continue.

"Anything you say can be used against you in a court of law."

"Exactly. Anything you say can and certainly will be used against you in a court of law. Of course, it is the court of Alejandro's cousin. And, an attorney will be provided for you. I have a cousin who is an attorney. Of course, we do not have much violent crime on our little island so he may not be very good, and he is more fond of Concepción than the judge. He is her great uncle, but that is all that is available. Now, do you understand these things?"

Creature shook his head in silent agreement, eyes so wide with understanding I thought they'd fall out.

"Now, I have a few questions for you. I do hope

you will cooperate. The young lady your accomplices apparently kidnapped is also my most favorite cousin."

"I say nothing," he snapped, but then looked over the burly police officer's shoulder. I was hefting the torch and acting as if to light it.

"Oh, I am sorry to hear that. If you will you excuse me a moment, I need to step outside. Too much tea this afternoon. And then I must radio the office again."

"No!" creature screamed. "Don't leave me alone with these crazy people!"

"Nonsense. Relax. I won't be long, but reception was not very good the last time I was here, so probably will have to drive several miles from here for the radio to work properly. These fine, upstanding citizens will take good care of you," he answered, patting our victim's leg.

The creep suddenly got very talkative. Lt. Carlos settled back next to him and wrote vigorously, occasionally getting translation help from Josh.

"Well, I believe that is about all for now," Carlos said as Papa Vasquez entered the cave. "If you young men would untie the bindings I shall take him to jail. Ah, Profesor Vasquez, so glad you arrived. And Señorita Calderõn. This is not a very nice place for a young lady."

"She came to tell me what happened and insisted upon returning," Papa answered. "Are you boys alright?"

"Yes. It looked pretty bad until Isabella and Josh showed and he took this guy out."

"Oh, that wasn't me. That was the señorita," Josh explained.

"I have much work to do," the police officer said. "If you would take these young gentlemen with you? They can tell you better than I what has happened. I am afraid it is not good. If I have further questions of my young cousins, I will contact you at the villa." Then taking Alejandro and me aside he whispered, "Please understand, to clear us of International liability I must put in my report the injuries were sustained during a struggle before I arrived. It is most unfortunate that he fell into a small campfire pit." He winked.

Sandwiched between Josh and Isabella, I struggled to put things together, one being Isabella.

"Josh said you took out that creature."

"At the school I attend in Spain, the headmaster believes that we young ladies should know how to defend ourselves. I have studied Karate for a number of years." She giggled behind a hand. "I like beating up boys."

"Thanks for the warning."

"Oh, I would never do something like that to my favorite dance partner."

Once back at the villa, Alejandro and I showered. Far too keyed up, the family physician administered a sedative. He'd come to check out the cuts to our feet. Try as we might to stay awake, Alejandro and I collapsed into our respective beds. Sometime during that fitful sleep, the strange dream from earlier reoccurred. About mid-morning the next day, we both woke about the same time to rush downstairs to find out about Concepción.

"They could not find the boat," Señor Vasquez said.

"What do you mean they couldn't find the boat? It was big and white! It would stand out like an iceberg!" I shrieked. My head began to pound viciously as tears blurred my vision, abating only after some time on Grandma's shoulder and a warm cup of tea.

Chapter 9

The Canary Island Commandos

Themselves grieving, Papa Vasquez, Grandma, and Aunt Herminia spent the day consoling us, silently worrying I was over wrought by the whole ordeal. They weren't aware how over wrought I had become the day before with a blowtorch. Alejandro wasn't much better, but there was nothing we or anyone else could do. The simple fact was that somehow a great big, white yacht with our sister aboard simply disappeared.

A couple days later one of the villagers from the fishing village where we initially head to seek refuge, reported that a big, white boat came to pick up the man who had come in a rubber boat looking for us. Later that day word arrived that a boat fitting the description was seen off Puerto de la Cruz on the west side of Isle of Tenerife the afternoon after Sis was abducted. Obviously, her captors turned south after leaving Dolphin Cove to pick up their man, and then continued around the tip of El Hierro and north along the western coast. We assumed they would immediately head for the African coast sixty some miles east. Everyone had been searching in the wrong direction.

The same day that revelation came forth, we received word that a Spanish military ship intercepted a yacht by the name and description broadcast to authorities as it passed Gibraltar heading into the Mediterranean. Concepción was not aboard. Although everything matched, they asked if we were certain it could be the same boat. Boarding a plane for Spain, Alejandro, Papa, Grandma, and I arrived in Marbella on the Spanish Mediterranean coast to make positive identification.

Taking no chances of provoking an international incident, the police presented the yacht's crew in a lineup intermingled with local Italians living there. It was difficult. Most of those we saw had been from a distance, or a blur while trying to escape, or during our capture. Alejandro thought to recognize a couple, but couldn't be a hundred percent certain. The same with me. There were two we positively identify—creature being held in custody on El Hierro, and . . . the leader who stepped last onto the viewing platform.

"That's him!" we shouted together.

"He was giving all the orders at the hacienda," Alejandro explained.

I would not soon forget his arrogant, smug expression. Even face to face, he retained a cool, aloof attitude of innocence. After all, we were just a couple excited children.

"May I speak with him alone?" I asked. "I promise not to kill him."

The chief investigator smiled. Little did he know what I was capable. Agreeing, the two of us were brought together in a room with two-way mirrors, a microphone, and lots of people secretly taking in the meeting.

"I'm curious. Why did you cut out and leave that moron guarding us? You must have known he would kill us before trying to escape the island."

He said nothing, just smiled faintly. That sent a shiver down my spine. That had been his intent, and why leaving ahead of schedule. He wanted to be rid of him and us, and not have his conscious bothered.

"Well, obviously he didn't. That was a mistake on your part, you know. Before the police arrived to arrest him he said many things, important things."

The boss gestured with one hand to indicate, "Such as?"

"Who you are, where you are from, where they are taking my sister, how many guards are normally used both going to the cave and in the cave, who your patriarch is, who gave the order to kidnap me, and why Concepción was a much better choice."

His eyes narrowed to glowering slits.

"Let me fill you in on some details." I then lowered my voice to a bare whisper. The name you gave the police is a lie. You are Raffaele De Stefano, a capodecina, or a boss. You run your own family with ten soldiers. Actually, you only have nine with the loss of that idiot you left to kill us. Your boss is Paolo Rosario De Stefano of the 'Ndrangheta di Calabria. Your brother, Giovanni, runs his own family. Together, you operate a lucrative kidnap for ransom scheme. Your headquarters is on a hill overlooking a little fishing village a bit north of Scilia, and the cave you hold your prisoners is about twelve miles northeast of there in the mountains of the Aspromonte."

His eyes got wider and wider as I counted off the details. Finally, trying to recoup his composure, said, "You are a person with much misinformation. How does one of your tender years come up with all this – this imaginary story?"

"Ever watch American westerns?"

"Yes."

"Where the Indians stake a prisoner out over an ant hill? Well, there weren't any ants in the cave, but there was a plumber's torch. Amazing how quickly it helps a person to sing, especially high notes. Now, because I have all this information, I will suggest the police let it be known it came from you."

His coppery complexion nearly turned albino.

"I don't need anything from you, actually. The police will feel very proud to have arrested such a notorious criminal. I just want you to know we got your number, slime ball, and I'll just let your compatriots do the rest. Revenge can be sweet," I said, getting up to leave him alone at the table.

Several hours later, an investigator came to our hotel room to report the yacht captain would not divulge any information, and wanted to know what had passed between us. I had spoken too low to be heard.

"Have you a plumber's torch?"

The officer looked at me genuinely puzzled. I then handed him a large envelope with the incriminating details derived from the creep on El Hierro. Missing were specifics of the place our sister was held, vaguely mentioning the district of Reggio Calabria in Italy's toe.

"Just let it be known this came from him. That should do the trick."

Feeling pleased with that orchestration, I settled into bed. Almost immediately, the reoccurring dream fired up. This time it was crystal clear. Awaking with a start, I sat up, coming face to face with the Captain sitting on the end of my bed.

"It happened to you, didn't it?" I asked, knowing the answer. "You mentioned it in your journal. How Hassan was kidnapped and you went to his rescue."

"Yes."

"I'm going to rescue Concepción. Will you help?"

"I would dissuade you from such a dangerous undertaking."

"Will you help?"

As much as I can, but understand, Francis, I cannot stress that such an undertaking will be dangerous. Very dangerous. You have no experience in such things. I did."

"I'm an Evreux. We laugh in the face of danger. You said that," I replied.

"I was young and reckless."

"Another family trait. So am I."

"Is something wrong?" Alejandro mumbled as he propped himself on one elbow in the bed next to mine.

I proceeded to unfold the crazy idea hatching in my mind. Surprisingly Alejandro agreed. Well before dawn, we sneaked out of the hotel and headed for the marina to charter a boat. We were head for Italy to rescue Concepción ourselves. Of course, we couldn't charter just any boat, it had to be a boat with a captain willing to help and not toss us overboard after putting to sea. In finding such a man, we relied on my ancestor.

"The man who owns that boat would be honest in giving you aid," he said, pointing to a thirty-foot, charter fishing boat.

Standing on the dock in a dark, chilly fog we stared at a two-masted, wood boat. A shiver ran down my back. It looked exactly like the one in my dreams.

"So, now what?" Alejandro asked softly.

"I guess we find the captain and ask."

"And what would you ask me?" a deep, baritone voice boomed out of the dark from behind us. We both jumped, nearly pitching into the water.

"We wish to charter your ship, sir," I stuttered.

"It is a boat, son, not a ship, though it is grand enough. So you wish to charter a fishing trip?"

"Ah-h, no, not exactly a fishing trip. Something a little longer," Alejandro replied.

"How long?"

"We need to go to Italy?" I said with some hesitation.

He cast about nervously and then said, "It is chilly out here. Let's go aboard, have some coffee, and talk."

The single, rear deck cabin was more spacious than I guessed. Seated on an L-shaped, cushioned bench wrapping around a small table, my hands shook as they grasped the hot cup of black Turkish coffee, not from cold but fear. I wasn't sure how he would respond, but then the Dolphin had guided our footsteps to this particular boat.

"We are from the Island of El Hierro in the Canary Islands," Alejandro began to explain. "A few days ago some men, Mafia guys, kidnapped our sister and took her to Italy."

"We are told she will be held for ransom," I added.

"We came here to identify the men who did it. The Spanish government caught their yacht, but she was not aboard," Alejandro finished.

The wind-burnt skipper stroked his grizzled,

salt and pepper stubble thoughtfully before saying, "You are from El Hierro? What are your
names?"

"I am Alejandro Vasquez-Albarez and he is David Dolphene-Evreux."

"Did you say Evreux?"

"Yes, sir."

"You wouldn't happen to be a descendant of
Francois Evreux, the . . . ah . . . merchant sailor?"

"Yes, sir," I answered, strangely feeling more
confident. "I am a direct descendant."

"That is interesting. Very interesting. How did
you happen to come to find this particular boat to
charter for what is a foolish rescue mission?"

"A friend," is all I would answer. Let's be real
here. Who would accept the idea two kids being
guided by a ghost?

"My family is well acquainted with the Evreux
family. A story has been passed from generation
to generation until becoming a vague legend con-
cerning a distant relative with the same name as I,
Santana."

Suddenly, like a voice speaking to my mind,
came the answer. I blurted it out. "Your ancestor
was an officer under my ancestor, the pirate
known as the Dolphin!"

"Yes. That is the story," he replied in shock.
"But how did you . . .?"

"Captain Santana, I don't know how to explain
this," I began, faltering. "Do you believe in ghosts?"

His dark face paled dramatically.

"We would have never thought to attempt

such a foolish rescue, as you put it, if we didn't have some help."

"A ghost?"

"Yes, sir. Captain Evreux, the Dolphin. He knew who you were and directed our feet to this ship, I mean boat."

The captain slumped back in his seat and stared at us for a long time. "You know what you propose is crazy beyond words." Then a grin spread across his weathered face. "If the Dolphin has come back from the dead to help you in this misadventure, then by all that is holy, or unholy, I shall see you to Italy!"

Capt. Santana's boat was a Mediterranean workhorse, a Tirhandil. The centuries-old, Aegean Double Ender design kept it to under fifty feet with two masts, using a bow sprit and lanteen sails, somewhat similar to the Raven, my ancestor sailed. Of course, it had undergone some modernization to provide amazing comfort for short, tourist cruising.

When the captain fired up the engine, the boat vibrated and rumbled like an awaking dragon, but upon entering open water within the hour, he directed us to raise the sails and then cut the engine. The sudden silence was profound as all we heard was the water rushing past as the bow sliced through the gentle swells.

After showing Alejandro how to pilot the boat, Capt. Santana took me below to help prepare breakfast in the large galley. It was then I learned this was more than just a charter fishing boat.

"When I was a boy, not much older than you, I became involved with the wrong sorts. Sicilians. At first it was very exciting, but then bad things happened. We were in a warehouse and the police came. We were surrounded and out numbered. There was shooting. Lots of confusion. I had much fear, as you are experiencing now." My shivering was pretty obvious. Handing me a jacket, casually buttoning it up as my fingers would not cooperate. "I ran, and then something told me to climb. The top of the crates were perhaps fifteen meters. It was difficult, but I made it to the top just in time and lay flat, barely breathing as the police searched for us. I alone went undetected. As the sun began to bring light into the building, everyone left. It was so quiet, I could hear my heart beating, and then the voice that told me how to hide said for me to move to the back of the building. There I found a sewer cover and escaped. Disgusting, but I lived. The others did not do so well. Those who died that night were the lucky ones. Prison is a stalking death.

"The sewer emptied into the harbor. I swam ashore and sat upon the rocks not knowing what to do. I had no clothes but those I wore and they were covered with filth, and then a man suddenly appeared and sat next to me."

"You are in trouble," he said. It was not a question. I did not answer, but only stared at him. He smiled. "You are the first person I have ever seen born into this world through a sewer pipe."

He never asked, but the trouble that night at

the warehouse was common knowledge. All that shooting does not go unnoticed.

"That is my boat," he said, pointing to a boat much like my Genevieve, but not so fine." Santana laughed. "It was a rust-eaten wreck on the verge of its last voyage. Or at least that is the way it looked."

"I could use some help," he said. "If you are interested in sailing from this place, swim over and come aboard on the far side when you see me row out."

"I have no papers," I told him.

"I have papers."

"He left and I waited. When I saw him go aboard, I swam out. He was standing at the rail, smoking a pipe, waiting."

"Before I throw down a rope, get rid of those filthy rags," he said. When I was naked, he tossed down a bar of soap so that I could bathe. You cannot believe how good it felt to be clean. I have bathed every day since. Anyway, I came aboard, he provided clean clothes, food, and papers. He was very good at that . . . forging documents. I went to sea with him under the name of Monello." The captain laughed again. "It means brat." His laughter eased my fear and tension.

"The man was a smuggler among other things. He treated me as a son. We were together for many years and did well until he retired. I took over the trade and here I am, now the proprietor of a respectable cruise boat for hire. Of course, there are a few transactions on the side. It is a hard habit to break, and it helps to pay the bills when customers as scarce. So, tell me about your plans."

"Our sister is being held in a cave in the mountains of southern Italy, somewhat north of Regio di Calabria near a fishing village north of Scilia."

Ah, yes. I am familiar with where you speak."

"They left one of their kind behind to guard us. With a little help, we got free and he told us about the cave, distance from the village, number of guards on the way, and inside."

"And you believed him?"

"Yes. He was very talkative."

"Interesting. They take an oath, *omertà,* the code of silence. To break that oath is to die."

"Frankly, not to speak meant being barbecued an inch at a time with a blowtorch," I replied firmly.

He arched a bushy eyebrow. "I see. So, you plan to walk right into this cave and escort your sister out."

I stumbled. There were some details lacking.

"You two need serious help. Can you shoot a pistol? No? Alright. You obviously have no other clothes. You are so unprepared you will be dead the minute after your feet touch Italian soil."

Going to a padded seat along the bulkhead, the captain removed the back cushion revealing a hidden compartment. From this, he extracted a leather pouch fastened with a bit of leather cord. Digging into its musty depths, he extracted a folded piece of paper about eight inches square. Carefully opening it over the table, he spread out a map of the area where they supposedly had taken Concepción. The map was faded, dog-eared, and looked every bit of a hundred years old, still, it was a start. "A little something from the old days," is all he said.

From Marbella we sailed east 400 nautical miles, timing our arrival at Port d'Andraty on west coast of the island of Mallorca near sunset thirty-six hours later. In our hurry, we had failed to take our passports, which was just as well. Capt. Santana provided some with mis-information. We remained aboard as he went ashore, returning before midnight somewhat inebriated. That morning he took us on a shopping spree so that we would look like real crew—trousers, stripped tee shirts, and black deck shoes. We also purchased black trousers, black, long sleeve turtlenecks, and black stocking caps. The acquisition of hundreds upon hundreds of balloons was a curiosity. Purchases arranged in an alley behind a small, dingy restaurant were two .32 cal. automatic pistols with shoulder holsters and what I thought was a lot of ammo. The final acquisition was a small, rubber raft and paddles.

I offered to reimburse him, but he correctly said, "The minute you access your bank account everyone will know where you are and put an end to this misadventure. Besides, I owe this to your ghostly companion."

Restocked, refueled, and equipped, we set a course for Caligari on the island of Sardinia. During that two day leg the captain spent a lot of time teaching us everything there was to know about our pistols, especially how to break them down and clean each part. The amount of ammo was not excessive, either, as we did a lot of target practice, shooting balloons bobbing on the water. We came to be fairly proficient at hitting the moving targets.

"There is a rule you must set in your minds. When someone wants to shoot at you, do not hesitate for even a fraction of a second to shot back, preferably first, and shoot to kill. To not do this, you will be dead."

That sobering advise left us shaken. The thought of taking another life was disturbing. Alejandro and I lie in our bunks whispering as Capt. Santana took the midnight to four A.M. Watch.

"I do not think it will be possible for me to shoot someone," my brother said.

"I don't know, either."

"Capt. Santana is correct," a voice said, startling both of us that we nearly baled from beneath the sheets. My ancestor sat on the foot of my bed.

Recapturing both our wits and heartbeats, Alejandro said, "But it is against God's law to take another life."

"When Abraham went to rescue his nephew Lot, do you not think that men were not killed in that battle? Moses killed an Egyptian. David killed Goliath. The prophet Samuel told King Saul that it was the will of the Lord that he destroy the Amalekites, both male and female, adult, child, and infant. Saul failed to do that, and the Lord rejected him. Samuel then took a sword and killed Agag. Were any of these men condemned? So the Lord has given a commandment." He reached to a small shelf of books above my head and took down the Holy Bible. Thumbing directly to a page near the beginning, he continued. "In the Book of Leviticus, chapter 19, verse 16, it says that you shall not stand against the blood of thy neighbor. That means if someone is threatened with physical violence, you are required to come to their defense to the best of your ability. That goes for protecting yourself as well. Think on what I have said. Your mind must not be hampered by waiting to decide what course of action to take. Otherwise, return home, and pay the ransom."

"But you are here instead of in Heaven because you killed," Alejandro protested.

"There is a difference between protecting one's self and others, and murder. I murdered."

With that declaration, the Captain was gone. We I looked at one another, rolled onto our backs, and drifted into a fitful slumber each giving thought upon what was said.

At Caligari we refueled and headed across the Tyrrhenian Sea straight for the Italian boot arriving off-shore of Scilia at the northern mouth to the Strait of Messina. The afternoon was spent 'fishing.' By this time I was so nervous the slightest noise and I would have been as airborne as Winnie the Pooh's marmalade friend, Tigger.

"There is no reason to go ashore too early. Get some rest," Santana said.

Yeah. Rest. I lay staring at the ceiling. So did Alejandro because I didn't hear his usual, nocturnal snores. We heard Captain Santana in the galley as the aroma of one of his favorite Greek meals drifted throughout the boat. Finally came his footsteps on the gangway.

"Now that you have not slept and are thoroughly exhausted, it is time to eat, which you probably will not do so to become weak and incapable of lifting a finger to help your sister," he said.

He was right. We hadn't slept well the whole trip, not at all this day, and just stared at the food, despite not only looking good, but smelling wonderful.

"You are not hungry because you are frightened. That is natural, but force yourself. It may be a long time before you eat again," he said. "Besides, it is not good to die on an empty stomach." His encouragement was not really helpful, but we forced ourselves to eat.

Changing into the black clothing, and painting the back of our hands and faces black, we prepared to go ashore. Capt. Santana used a muffled motor to edge us with a half mile of shore. Using an on-board air pump the raft was inflated and slipped over the side.

As we lowered into the raft he said quietly, "Farewell my young friends. Here is a small radio. If the gods and your great ancestor manage to somehow get you through this crazy scheme, call me. I will be fishing along the coast line."

"Thank you Capt. Santana. I don't know how we could have gotten this far without you," I said.

"You would not have. Do not spoil your tremendous run of luck by getting caught or shot." With those encouraging words, we began rowing. "Don't listen to an old flounder like me. You will do fine," he called after us as we disappeared into a moonless night, and then I think he uttered a blessing or prayer.

While patrolling the coastline, fishing poles out, we spotted the little, coastal village of Scilia and private marina with a number of expensive boats and a sizable yacht. High up on a hill, a fancy villa stood sentinel-like nestled among a forest of olive trees. We navigated using those lights.

I knew Alejandro's stomach was knotted as tight as mine was when he made a nervous joke, "I think to have seen this scene in a James Bond movie."

"Yeah. Well, look out Italy, here come the Canary Island Commandos," I joked back.

Chapter 10

The Invasion

Our adventure certainly mimicked a scene from a Bond DVD. Rolling ashore on a wave, we deflated the raft and hid it among rocks well up the beach from the village. A compressed canister of air would almost instantly re-inflate it upon our return. The intention was to work our way inland to the road leading to the cave. James Bond had movie lights to illuminate the way. We had nothing, and very quickly discovered our folly of thinking it would be an easy walk in the dark. Imagine being in total dark, wearing a blindfold, and trying to negotiate uneven terrain. After banging into an unseen obstacle and doing a face-plant in the sand, we decided to hold up until pre-dawn light.

Sitting with knees drawn against my chest it

was impossible to see each other. Furthermore, we dared not speak so any patrols would not discover us. By this time one or the other should have wised up and realized we were just a couple stupid kids acting out a fantasy.

"This is stupid," Alejandro whispered after a long silence, unable to keep quiet. I think he wanted to hear a friendly voice as assurance. I did.

"I know."

"But we can't turn back, can we?"

"Yes . . . and no."

The momentum to continue was the Captain. We could see him walking up from the beach directly to where we sat. That was an eerie feeling, a hazy, faintly lighted figure moving through the blackness. My heart skipped a beat.

"It is him," Alejandro said, his voice was shaking, the first solid evidence he was a couple steps beyond scared. But then, both of us were a bit over-the-edge.

Coming up to stand feet spread apart, hands on hips, he said, "Scared?"

"Yes!" I answered.

"This is how it always feels, just before going into battle." He squat to be on eyelevel.

"I'm glad you came." He might not be able to shoot anyone, or hit them, but knowing he would be at hand was comforting and gave us courage.

"There is not much I can do to physically help you except offer a hand into the next world if you get killed."

"You and Capt. Santana are just full of encouragement," I grumbled.

"Just realistic. Something neither of you two seem to have a penchant for in this instance."

Up to this point we were using information that creep I barbecued in the cave generously provided, and I withheld from the police at the suggestion of the Captain. Now it all seemed buried in a blurry fog. I was in overload. Still, as the first hint of light made it possible to see where our feet stepped, we forged ahead. Admittedly, this part of the plan was hazy and not thought through very well. In fact, the whole plan was still hazy and not thought through despite Captain Santana's help and suggestions.

As the sky lightened, we reached a narrow, paved road climbing into the foothills. From this point Alejandro used our binoculars to check out a parking lot below the cliff upon which the villa stood overlooking the private marina.

"There are four cars and one of those stretch limos, and three motor scooters in the marina parking lot. Sure wish we could use a couple of those scooters."

"Any guards?"

"Four."

"Not likely they'll let us borrow them."

"The *cabrón* in the cave back home said they change guards every morning," Alejandro said. "Let's sneak up the road a ways and ambush the riders when they came our way." That seemed a plausible plan.

At nine, it was still relatively comfortable, but as the sun moved higher, it beat down with an intensity that soaked into our black outfits. While watching the parking lot we sweltered among the rocks a half mile inland, waiting less patiently than when first arriving.

"This once was a fertile forest before the Romans cleaned it out," the Captain said as he waited with us, lounging on his back, head resting on a round rock, feet crossed, hands folded over his chest. He looked way too comfortable and relaxed.

"I wish they had left at least one tree for shade," I retorted.

My eyes began to hurt as they strained through the small binoculars as if trying to send a message for someone to hurry up and do something other than stand around and talk. Finally, there was activity in the parking lot as two guys actually prepared to leave on scooters.

As they roared up the narrow trail-road, Alejandro lay on the edge. As hoped, they stopped, guns at the ready to check out the intruder. Simultaneously the Captain and I appeared from behind a big rock brandishing pistols as Alejandro rolled over pointing his. Of course, the Captain had two, not that they would have done any good, but our captives didn't know that.

Frankly, I was amazed how easy it had been. Taking them well off the road, we took their clothes, and bound them with duct tape. Their clothes fit Alejandro okay. I was at least six inches taller and felt like a silly school boy with a wedgie and high-waters, but there was no time for tailoring.

Leaving the guards bound and stashed, we slipped on their helmets, mounted the scooters, and headed up the road. I assumed the Captain would follow by whatever means he used to get around. According to the information readily given by the dirt bag on El Hierro, the turnoff was about five miles from where we started. There would be a guard stationed at the intersection. I actually felt a sense of relief when they hove into view. A feeling that the information could be wrong continually nagged my conscious, but so far, everything he told us continued to pan out.

Upon seeing us, the two next to a pickup truck merely waived as we turned off onto the side road. The dark colored visors on the helmets helped greatly. Another eight miles further, we came to the cave entrance. There were two vehicles in the open space by the entrance, a pickup and a four door van. Again, we encountered a couple guards, but they were equally casual and simply waived as we parked. It was our, or rather the job of those we intercepted, to relieve them. This we did, of their weapons and dumped them bound and gagged with duct tape into the box of the pickup. So far, so good, but this was all the information we had. From here, we would have to wing it. I neglected to get detailed information about the inside of the cave. I was really kicking myself for that oversight, but Alejandro was equally guilty.

Inside the cave, we followed a man-enhanced tunnel until reaching a fork. Footprints in the soft dirt went both ways so we split up, Alejandro taking the right. Several hundred yards down the left passage, it opened into a large room. It seemed extremely well lit. Peeking around a corner, I saw the reason, a floodlight. Someone was making a video. The subject was a tall, skinny guy, with no more than a towel wrapped around his waist, kneeling on the ground in front of the camera, hands tied behind his back. I watched as two guys huddled around the camera, fiddling with the thing. Finally, they seemed to have resolved whatever problem they had and one stepped into the light to stand behind the prisoner. My mouth fell open. How could he be here?

Chapter 11

Concepción's Ordeal

Concepción wasn't about to cooperate when the gangsters abducted her, but despite her strength there was no way to struggle against the weightlifter who seemed to know all her tricks to escape, or he was impervious to pain. As soon as her brothers disappeared inside the hacienda a second injected a drug into her shoulder. Within seconds, it took effect. Tossed over the gorilla's shoulder like a sack of rice, the journey became blurred after entering the forest, and then the world went dark.

Time became a fuzzy jumble as she drifted in and out of consciousness, vaguely remembering being required to change into men's pajamas before getting off a boat, being driven in a car, and then being on an airplane. When the plane landed, she was more cognizant of the surroundings. It must have been a private airstrip as there were no other planes around. A car trip to the ocean was relatively short where they boarded another boat. Less than half a day on water they disembarked where a SUV whisked her through a forest of some sort into rugged mountains to the mouth of a mine.

The tunnel they entered was cool compared to outside. After walking a ways, they escorted her through a very large cavern. It was then she realized this was a cave, not a mine. Crossing the large chamber, they entered another tunnel on the opposite side. Shortly they came to a room about the size of a small house appointed much like a primitive dormitory with simple, iron-frame beds. There was a lavatory behind a curtain, providing little in the way of privacy.

Releasing her bonds, the guard closed the door in the iron bar grill-work spanning the entrance and laughed. "Make yourself to home, Señorita, and entertain yourselves. You two are old enough to know how to do that." She hated his disgusting laugh, as it seemed to echo endlessly as he disappeared down the tunnel. Turning, she looked at her cellmates, both boys.

Standing next to one another, they looked the extreme of a Mutt and Jeff cartoon. Next to a towering young man, the child looked so tiny. As she would learn much later, he was a small ten-year-old. Both dressed in pajamas and no slippers as she, they appeared gaunt and haggard, but the fear in the child's eyes gripped her heart. Neither said a word as she cast about the room.

There were four beds. The two furthest back each had a blanket piled on them. The two nearest the door each had a folded blanket next to a pillow.

"Hallo," the young man said. "Sind Sie Deutscher?"

Concepción canted her head slightly, not understanding him.

"Wo kommst du her?"

"No entiendo. I do not understand," she said in Spanish and English, silently praying they spoke a common language.

"My Spanish not so goot. English ist better. My name ist Franz Galfridus. This ist Lauro. He ist Italian, but I do not know much more. He does not speak. Only cry."

"My name is Concepción Vasquez. I am from the Island of El Hierro in the Spanish Canary Islands. Where is this place?"

"Somewhere in Italy, I think. That ist all they speak here. I really do not know. The last I remember war drinking with friends at disco on the *Bleichstraße* in meine city of Frankfurt. There war a dream of going somewhere until waking up here."

She walked to the first bed and sat down, totally distraught. Looking toward the dimunitive child, she reached out a hand. Taking one slow step after another, he came to stand by her. Patting the mattress at her side, he sat, whereupon she wrapped an arm around his bony body. He instinctively snuggled close. The German boy sat on the dirt floor, back against the rock wall.

"Do you know what is going on? Why are we here?"

"These men are criminals, what ist called mafioso. They take children of important people and hold für ransom. Meine vater ist banker in Frankfurt, very wealthy. I have been here five months now. I know how long because I make mark on der wall like so many before. Lauro war brought here two weeks ago. From what guard say, his vater ist important man in der Italienisch government. I do not think they want money für him. Something else."

"How old are you Lauro?" she asked in passible Italian.

The boy turned his head up to look at her briefly, and then resumed a bowed posture, saying nothing."

"I think he ist nine or ten," Franz answered. "He does not make any sound except I hear him cry during der nacht."

Concepción tightened her grip to reassure the boy.

Franz was quite tall, she guested at least six foot-two and slender. Besides appearing pale and haggard, she found him handsome. Green eyes peered from behind a wall of wavy, flaxen hair hanging to the base of his neck where it curled upward. Although disheveled, it complemented a narrow, oval face with a strong jaw tapering to a slightly squared chin. A slightly flared nose dropped from dark eyebrows to overhang a generous mouth with thin lips.

"How old are you?" she asked .

"I will be eighteen in two weeks. I will probably not live that long. Meine vater has been stubborn about paying. The last communication said that if he does not pay three million Euros I will be killed."

Concepción gasped. She somehow knew these people meant what they threatened. The third morning a commotion swept into the room just beyond their prison. A few minutes later three guards herded the captives from their cell into the great room. In the middle knelt a man in military-style camos, hands bound behind his back, face beaten and bloodied. A floodlight illuminated the scene for a video camera to focus on the new captive.

"It would seem your father is to play the fool. He sent men to rescue you. This one is the only survivor," the man who always wore a sport suit jacket, but no tie explained. "You, kneel beside him," he ordered. Donning a ski mask, he stood behind them and nodded for the cameraman to begin.

"Herr Galfridus, you are a fool," he said. "You send men to rescue your son instead of money. They have failed. This one survived."

Then to Concepción's horror he produced a pistol, pointed at the man's head and fired. The body pitched forward. Moving the barrel to Franz's head he continued, "The price is now six million Euros. If it is not paid in seven days I will pull the trigger again. The clock ticks."

Concepción and Franz were traumatized, but not so much as Lauro. She remembered issuing a short cry as the little boy curled his quaking body around her hips. Returned to their quarters, he began sobbing uncontrollably. Franz sat in one corner, knees drawn to chest, his whole body shuddering violently, too frightened to cry, although he desperately wanted to. When Lauro finally collapsed from sheer exhaustion, Concepción settled him onto his cot, and then went to Franz.

With a dampened cloth, she cleaned the dried blood from his face, "Remove your pajamas. I will wash them."

"He won't pay," he said stoically, stripping them off without standing and tossing them roughly on the ground.

"Surely he will," she replied scrubbing away at the dried blood that had splattered on his clothes.

"He only sent those men to appease meine mutter. I am embarrassment to him. He hates me."

"But why?"

"I am gay," he replied almost vehemently, faltering slightly as he spoke.

Concepción stopped scrubbing and stared.

Franz Linfreid Galfridus could have been a German centerfold heart-throb. The roots of his hair were black spilling out in long strands. For something to do several days earlier, she brushed out the tangles and tied it into a ponytail much like David's. That's when she notice the brilliant blue stud in his left ear. The only other jewelry he wore were a braided leather chocker with a paddle-shaped, brown stone pendant, and three, woven cord anklets. The stud they probably didn't see or would have taken. It was lapis lazuli, a rare, brilliant blue stone sought for thousands of years. The others were not expensive, probably why they allowed him to keep them. With nothing more than a white tank top and boxers, he drew his knees tight against his chest to bury his face on them. She thought to detect him silently crying. Sitting next to him, she put an arm around his shoulders. They quivered slightly.

After a time, he lift his head and leaned it back against the rough rock wall. His eyes were bloodshot. "This is perfect way to be rid of me. He shall say he tried to rescue me, and may even claim to have attempted to pay, und act very sad, but in his heart he will be glad."

There was nothing Concepción could think to respond. They sat together, her arm around his shoulders. That seemed to give him comfort. It did for her. The next day he became totally withdrawn and spoke not a word. Although clean, he refused to wear the pajamas, remaining in his underwear. Their captors came only to bring food at which time Lauro fled into Concepción's arms and trembled violently. None of their captors spoke to them except one. Not much older than Franz, he always made comments.

"Six days remain. I hope your papa does not pay. It would be very pleasurable to watch you die," he taunted, walking away, his psychotic laughter filling the room until disappearing. Returning the next day he said, "Five days remain. I hope your papa does not pay. It would be very pleasurable to watch you die. We will send your papa a hand so he knows we keep our word. *Il capo* says I can do that. Maybe I remove other things as well."

When the boy brought their food the seventh evening, he closed the door and turned the key. She knew what was coming.

"Your papa did not pay. Tomorrow, it will be very pleasurable to watch you die. Perhaps they will let me do it. I am not so quick about such things. I would use my knife and . . ."

Concepción heaved her bowl of food, splattering him. He stared at her a moment, snarled, and began unlocking the door.

"Come on you slimy, misbegotten animal," she said, taking a defensive stance Josh had shown her during their beach outings. "Come and we shall see who loses what part of their body."

The young man stopped with the door partially open, looked down the tunnel, then glared at her a moment longer, thinking.

"Well, big, brave, gutless creature. Afraid of a girl, you . . ." she unleashed another epithet that would curl the toes of even not-so-polite society.

He seemed frozen, one hand on the bars, the other on the key still in the lock.

"What's wrong, you greasy-looking, pimple-faced, dog's rear?" To really emphasize the taunt, she laughed. "Look who's afraid of the big, bad girl, the big bad girl, the big bad girl." The words were put to the melody sung by the Three Little Pigs.

He flung the door open. What pea brain didn't realize when he came within a three feet of Concepción, she owned him, knife or no knife, he was dead meat. However, before he could step into the cell a hand reached out and slammed the door shut.

"Get yourself cleaned up and go down the hill," the boss said.

"I want to teach her respect," the boy whined.

The man's hand slapped him so hard his head spun sideways and bang into the bars. "I know about this girl. She would more than teach you respect and then they would escape. Get out of my sight before I decide to let her practice on you." Grabbing his shirt collar, he propelled the whimpering child down the tunnel. Turning to stare at Concepción, his anger was piqued. "You will get no more food this night."

"Why? Afraid what I may do with it?"

He chuckled softly. "Yes." Locking the door, he turned and left.

When she awoke the next morning, Franz sat against the wall as usual, wearing a towel. His father had not paid as expected. As they came, he stood as complacent as a cow going to slaughter. The leader who had pulled the trigger on Franz's rescuer entered first. As they bound his hands behind his back, the leader looked at him questioningly and then toward the cot he occupied. His underwear lay on the ground thrown in a heap against the wall.

"You wish to die in a towel?" the boss asked,

puzzled.

"I come into this world mit nothing. I will leave mit nothing, especially if it war purchased by the man who thought to call himself meine vater."

"My own son would have been your age had he lived. Pablo and his mother were killed by government police sixteen years ago. I would hope he would have been as brave as you."

"Would you think any less of him if he were gay?"

The man faltered before replying, "It would have been a hard thing to accept, but I could not have loved him any less."

As a tear seeped from Franz's eye, the man jerked his head sideways to indicate for the others to take him out. The leader paused, staring as he was led away, then said abruptly, "Enrico, this is your opportunity to be the star."

Enrico was the boy who had tormented Franz with his oily smiles and sadistic taunts. His brown eyes grew large as saucers as a huge grin of surprised pleasure parted his pockmarked face.

"Can I use my knife?" he almost squeaked with joy.

"No! Do as you have been told or you will join him," the man snapped.

Franz glanced over his shoulder. There was nothing Concepción could do or say except a simple "Good bye." She liked the tall, young man with the green eyes and blond mop, and began to cry as the horror of a week ago would be revisited. Lauro clung as if welded to her, quaking while sobbing uncontrollably.

"I am truly sorry this is to be done. He reminds me so of my Pablo. I shall not watch this time. You can understand."

Concepción responded as tears rolled down her cheeks, "I do not understand why he has to die?

"We must honor our word," he said coldly.

Some of the brilliant light filling the large cavern filtered down the short tunnel. A few minutes seemed like hours then a loud bang filled the cave. Concepción jerked, turning to stare at the passage where she last saw the German boy, a gasp of repulsion enveloping her whole body. Lauro jerked and squeezed so hard she thought he was trying to pull himself inside her body to escape this horrible world. Suddenly a smile spread across her smooth, brown face. The boss looked puzzled at the sudden change.

"Do you believe in guardian angels?" she asked, sounding defiant.

The man laughed. "Something for the weak-minded and desperate," he replied with a sneer.

"Well, you really should."

At that moment, the barrel of a pistol inched over his shoulder into view. Reaching forward she snatched the automatic pistol from the boss' shoulder holster. As the man slowly turned to face his captor, the most exquisite expression of consternation clouded his brown face. Before him stood a tall man dressed as if he had just stepped out of an American pirate movie pointing a flintlock pistol at him. Suddenly reaching out, he snatched his pistol from Concepción's hand and shot the Captain twice. The Dolphin grinned.

"You can't kill a guardian angel," she said.

Turning to flee, the last thing the mafioso boss remembered was the tripod holding the video camera. He did a perfect flip-flop as it repositioned his long, straight nose into something much broader and flatter. His legs and arms flipped up as his body flopped back, hitting the ground with a thud.

I was on the guy like an American calf roper on a steer, the dust from the impact of his landing still swirling up. Rolling him over roughly, I taped his hands and ankles together. As if being timed, I stood with hands held out to stop the clock.

"David!' Concepción squealed, throwing her arms around my neck and kissing me full on the lips.

Every young man should experience several things in life. One is the first kiss from a girl, not just a peck on the cheek, but a real kiss of passion on the lips. To have that happen when one is barely sixteen may be a bit early. It certainly put me in overload. Frozen in a petrified position of surprise, she shifted to Alejandro who came up from behind, greeting him lavishly, but not on the lips.

"It is alright," she finally explained to Lauro. "These are my brothers."

"We better get moving," Alejandro said. "Get your things."

"This is all we have. They killed the other . . . ?!" She stopped abruptly as the German stepped from the shadows. She attacked him, unabashedly, throwing her arms around his shoulders and kissing him on the cheek.

"Time enough for that later," the Captain announced. "You are not completely safe just yet."

"You can't go in a towel," Concepción said, tossing Franz the discarded pajamas, which he eagerly grabbed up. Slipping the bottoms on under his towel, he removed and folded it neatly, and bent down to tuck the material under the head of the boss with the rearranged face.

"He could have been a gūt vater," he said to Alejandro's questioned look.

"Then let's get out of here. Come on David," Alejandro barked.

Snapped from the stupor and uncurling toes, I leaped to bring up the rear as we hustled into the video room. However, we hadn't covered more than twenty feet when Alejandro unexpectedly came to a screeching halt, pointing his pistol at arm's length. Hurrying to the front, it was the guy I had shot just before he pulled the trigger on the German.

"How did he get here?" Alejandro asked as the guy stood transfixed, his glazed eyes trying to focus. The left side of his shirt was a mass of blood, hands still taped behind the back. "He's supposed to be in jail on El Hierro!"

That was my thought and perhaps why I hadn't hesitated to pull the trigger when he started to point his gun at me after the cameraman dropped following a love tap to his head. I unconsciously didn't want to kill him, however easy it would have been. Instead, I aimed for the tattoo peeking from beneath his shirt on the left side. Having become a marksman of sorts, I nailed it near dead center, knocking him to the ground. Before his intended victim realized the shot had not been for him and opened his eyes to find himself quite alive, I pounced on the would-be shooter and taped his hands. As Franz stood and stared in bewilderment, I bound the cameraman as well.

"He's always been here," Concepción answered.

"He has a twin," Franz said, "and just as crazy." Stepping up, he delivered a powerful, long-armed roundhouse to the guy's jaw sending him on a whirling face-plant into the dusty floor. "Ouch!" he said shaking his hand.

"Nice," I remarked.

"Are you alright?" Concepción asked.

"I never thought hitting someone would feel so goot. Stand him up. I want to do it again."

"Sorry, you have no time to play with your friend," the Captain said. "Better move along."

I understood later why he had as much hatred for this brother as I did for the other back on el Hierro, but another problem arose. Just at the edge of light, I saw movement.

"Look out!" I cried, sending everyone diving to the cave floor.

At that moment a red flash preceded an explosive boom. Alejandro and I returned fire, emptying a clip each. Reloading reflexively as trained, we charged the position from two sides.

"Whoever it was is gone!" Alejandro shouted.

"Whoever it was, I think we got him. There's blood," I said, wiping two fingers on a rock and looking at the red stuff.

"Come on. Get out before more guards show up." Coming to the entrance, Alejandro held up the train, checking to make sure no one else had arrived. "Looks clear. Still only two vehicles."

We had to take the pickup with the short box and four doors equipped with two bound guards trying vainly to get free in the back. It was the only one with keys in the ignition. Alejandro got behind the wheel. I crawled in next to him. The others jumped into the rear seats and we were off in a cloud of white dirt.

"Whoa! This has got some serious power," he beamed.

"Well, take it easy. Won't do us any good to crash. None of them have shoes for cross-country hiking," I said, my heart pumping for all it was worth, and wondering where the person we had exchanged shots with had gone.

Chapter 12

Escape

"Where are we going?" Sis asked, buckling up in the back seat and holding Lauro tightly, knowing her brother's penchant for erratic driving.

"To the coast. We have a boat waiting off shore," I answered.

Suddenly the rear window shattered. She screamed.

"Someone ist chasing us," Franz shouted while cowering to one corner in a tight ball as another bullet struck the tail gate. Concepción shoved Lauro to the floorboards.

"Where the heck did they come from?" Alejandro replied, trying to see the pursuing vehicle in the rear view mirror and watch the road at the same time.

"Probably the guy we shot at in the cave. Just

watch the road. We'll take care of this. Here, take this and shoot back," I said, handing Franz the pistol from Alejandro's shoulder holster.

"I have never used one of these."

"Just point and pull the trigger."

Franz did. The gun jumped. He flinched. Sis emitted a little yelp. Seeing the windshield of the pursuing vehicle hit, he felt better, and squeezed off a couple more rounds as the passenger in the SUV leaned out the side window to shoot again. A couple more quick rounds gave him reason to duck back inside quickly as their windshield starred again.

"Nice shooting."

Then a piece of the pistol dropped loose. "It broke!" he squealed.

"The clip's empty. Here, take this one," I said, trading pistols with him.

Unexpectedly a short-barreled rifle rose up into Concepción's hands. Pushed to the floor, Lauro found it attached to the bottom of the seat and passed it up. Taking it, she stared at it fearfully.

"Hot dog! A rifle," I crowed.

"What do I do with it?"

I was dumbfounded by the question. "What do you usually do with a rifle? Point it at the bad guys and pull the trigger."

"But I might hurt them."

I had no response. They were trying to kill us, her included, and she suddenly went peacenik. About then we heard more bullets hit the tailgate. One ripped through the top of her seat and destroyed the radio. In those few seconds Concepción looked at the hole inches from her left shoulder and at the console. Without further hesitation, she ran the rifle barrel out the shattered back window and squeezed the trigger. More than one round bullet spit out.

"Yes! A machine gun!" Alejandro yelled. "Let them have it!"

"You stop shooting at us," she yelled, letting fly another burst of shots. "Oh, darn, they quit chasing us."

Alejandro glanced in the rear view mirror. All he could see was a huge cloud of yellow-white dust.

"Do you think I hurt them?"

"Let God sort it out," I replied.

"We have more trouble," Alejandro announced.

Approaching the main road, the guards there had set up a roadblock with their vehicle. A bullet grazed the windshield creating a spray of lines. Franz didn't hesitate, shoving his pistol out the side window and firing, but the bullets went wild because of all the bouncing the truck was doing on the rough road. It was enough, though, to get them to leap for cover behind their vehicle as we arrived. Unable to turn left toward the ocean, Alejandro swung right, around a sharp curve, and into unknown territory, the guards quickly in pursuit.

The road became as serpentine as a spastic snake on caffeine so neither vehicle could get a clear shot at the other. Rounding a hairpin curve, our truck went into a harrowing slide. Amazingly, Alejandro managed to recover and accelerate down a long straightaway. Just as the pursuing truck appeared, Concepción fired a burst from the rifle. The truck continued its slide before flipping sideways and off the road into a shallow ravine.

"I think I hurt them, too," she said, not sounding nearly as concerned. "Where does this road take us?" she asked.

"Check the map, David," Alejandro answered, straining to see through the cracked windshield.

Pulling Santana's map from inside my shirt, I unfolded it. Several minutes passed before finding our location. "There's a small village north of here, but chances are it's controlled by that gang. How's the gas?"

"Full."

"Next intersection bear left. I think."

"That doesn't sound very confident," Concepción remarked.

"Hey, with this map I'm lucky to find Italy."

For the next hour, we crept along unknown, dirt roads weaving through the tortured terrain, following the questionable map, and beginning to feel easier until Concepción just had to ruin the moment as we crested a series of switchbacks up a steep mountainside.

"There are two vehicles down there. I think someone is following us again."

At the last curve, Alejandro floored it again on a straightaway. That's when it sounded like someone knocking on the roof followed by two holes in the hood and a series of dust bunnies popping up just ahead of our vehicle. Alejandro and I looked at each other a moment and then at the roof. There was a small, neat hole of light in the middle. Looking down at the side of my bucket seat, the edge was ripped next to my thigh. This revelation was followed by the roar of a helicopter streaking overhead to swing around and hang sideways just off the ground straight ahead.

"He is playing chicken. He expects you to swerve," Sis yelled.

"He expects to shoot us!" I hollered, clearly seeing a man in the open side door taking aim at us with a rifle.

In desperation I leaned out the window, took aim and opened fire until the clip ejected. Franz did the same on his side. It was enough. The man dove or fell back into the belly of the chopper as it made a sudden bank to get away. As we roared beneath, Alejandro clucked like a chicken. The accompanying maniacal laugh was a little disconcerting.

Concepción leveled the machine gun out the back window and let off a short burst. The chopper took off trailing a small stream of black smoke. It wasn't long before it was right back, though. It may have been damaged, but not enough to keep from giving chase. That gave Sis a good shot. Bracing the weapon on the back seat, she sighted down the barrel and squeezed off a short burst. The chopper veered away before going into a series of large circles before settling out of sight behind a hill. That was the last we saw of it.

"A car is gaining," she called up.

"You're just full of good news," I said.

"I can't go any faster on this road," Alejandro whined as we started down a steep, corkscrew road until hitting another longer, straight stretch through a narrow, forested valley.

I glanced at the speedometer. It read something over 140 kilometers per hour. I didn't know how fast we were really going, but it was scary, especially on a bumpy, dirt road with a totally inexperienced driver plastered with sweat, white knuckles glued to the steering wheel.

The pursuing vehicle closed within a hundred yards. Concepción took aim, waiting, obviously enjoying the newfound power. Being far better negotiating the numerous curves the pursuers rapidly gained on us as we began to climb out of the valley until within a couple hundred feet of the top. Rounding yet another bend they came into view long enough for her to fire a long-awaited burst of bullets. Just before we slowed to round the next curve, the vehicle swerved violently.

"Something black fly into der air off that car," Franz said. "I think it war part of der tire."

"Better them than us," Alejandro mumbled as sweat poured from his forehead.

"You okay?" I asked, not relishing the pressure he was enduring trying to drive way beyond his experience. Our lives were literally in his hands. His mouth was so dry he couldn't speak.

"Here comes the other one!" Concepción announced and fired a quick burst, but they kept coming. Then she just had to ruin everything. "I'm out of bullets."

"Is there another clip down there Lauro?" I asked, trying to look down between the front console. He shook his head, no.

"I've got an idea," Alejandro croaked as the car briefly came into view again allowing them to fire several shots. "Next curve I'm stopping. Everyone with loaded guns bail and open fire as they come around the curve."

The opportunity quickly became available. Alejandro slammed on the brakes allowing us to bail from the vehicle before it completely stopped. As the chaser roared around the curve, we opened fire. The natural reaction to swerve took them off the road and plummet into a ravine with a sickening, metallic roar. With Alejandro and Concepción standing ready for another vehicle, I eased over to the edge of the drop-off. The car was a mangled wreck. There was no movement from any occupants.

"Let's get out of here," I said, running back.

"No good, David," Alejandro said and pointed to the rear tire. It was shredded.

"Where's the spare?"

"It's not here," he continued with more uplifting news. "Maybe we can get one from them," and pointed to the wrecked car.

"We have another problem," Franz added to the growing list. "Your captives are dead."

Unbelieving, Alejandro and I looked in the pickup box.

"They must have been hit by the guy in the helicopter," Alejandro said.

"Well, better them than us," I replied sounding less sorry than I felt. "Can't do anything about that now. Alejandro, check the road. Franz, help me remove their shoes. You and Concepción need them more than they will."

"It's all clear for now," Alejandro reported as the two finished lacing up the boots.

"Okay, Franz, let's see if we can get down there and retrieve a spare. Alejandro, you and Sis stand guard."

The ravine in which the car plummeted was about thirty feet deep and a steep descent. The four inside were currently reporting to St. Peter, but the real disappointment was that all it's tires were ruined and it was impossible to retrieve the spare. The silver lining, albeit tarnished, was a compensating find. Fifteen minutes later, we regained the road loaded with guns and lots of ammo.

"Now what?" Concepción asked.

"Push the truck into the ravine. Anyone driving along here won't see either vehicle down there. We'll have to strike out on foot."

"What about Lauro. He doesn't have shoes," she protested.

"You guys carry the guns and ammo. Come on Lauro, time for a piggy-back ride."

"We cannot stay on der road," Franz said.

Just then, I spotted the Captain standing on the hill above us, motioning to come up, and pointing at something.

"Follow me," I said.

A narrow, animal trail lead up the hill where we could see a building some distance away, sufficiently off the road, and behind a small knoll, neatly secluded. Hiking as quickly as possible, we headed for what was an abandoned farm, keeping our ears tuned to any helicopter or airplane noises. Nearing the place, I cast a glance backward to see how the others were doing. It was a strange sight, three people heavily armed, two in pajamas, trekking across the open fields.

What must have been a barn was completely flattened from age. The house was not much more than a rock shell with great gaps in the walls and no roof. The one bright note was an artesian well around back supplying a small pond for the sheep grazing nearby.

"This is not going well, David," Alejandro whispered to me as we scouted the place. "They will get another helicopter in the air, and then they will see the wrecked cars in the ravine, and this place."

"Yeah, I know. I haven't a clue what we're going to do. I'm just too tired to think right now."

Alejandro returned to the house feeling equally discouraged. Standing alone and wondering why I had gotten us all into this mess, a voice said from behind, "Let them come to you." Spinning around, guns ready to fire, I came face to face with the Captain.

When my heart returned to its original spot allowing my vocal cords to function, I asked sarcastically, "And then what?"

"Take their vehicle."

Chapter 13

Someone Always Dies Tomorrow

As darkness gathered around our tiny group like a cloak to shelter us from searching eyes, there wasn't one person who didn't have a justifiable reason to complain. The temperature was cooling, we had no way to keep warm, no matches to start a fire, even if we dared, no food, and little hope for tomorrow. Despite all this, no one uttered a negative word as stomachs knotted, cramped, and growled with hunger. Lauro continued his silence while following me around to check out the farmstead and then snuggle close to Concepción with the onset of infinite blackness illuminated by the

Milky Way. The only thing keeping me buoyed was knowing the Captain was somewhere near. Sitting alone on a knoll used as our lookout, I was taking my turn at watch when he walked out of the dark.

"I love looking at the stars," he said softly, settling on the ground beside me, knees pulled up to his chest as were mine. "Many times I would sit on the bow of the Raven and stare at them for hours."

"I did that, too, at the lake back home in Nebraska, but I didn't realize how many there were until coming to El Hierro and getting away from the city lights. So many. So beautiful."

There was a long silence before he said, "Are you afraid of tomorrow?"

"Yes. As you said in your journal, the unknown can be frightening, but knowing you're close to protect us, not so much."

"That's not my job, Francis."

"Huh?"

"I am here to repent for my crimes, remember?"

"But you've been helping us," I protested.

"I can't protect you from dying. The best I can do is help you get to Heaven in better shape than me."

"Hey, this whole thing was your idea. So what are you saying? You set us up to get killed so we can go to Heaven?" I was understandably upset and on the verge of becoming unhinged from the stress. If I had any blood sugar, it was at the bottom of a very deep hole.

"Who sitting on this piece of dirt got the stubborn notion to pull off this stunt?"

"Why didn't you stop me?" The antithesis to his, my voice was loud, near shouting.

The captain continued, quiet and calm. "Francis, do you remember those two young men who came to your grandmother's house last January?"

I had to stop and think for a moment. "Yeah. Some preachers, ministers, something like that."

"Missionaries. Do you remember what they said about agency?"

I was so worked up, stopping to remember that visit was difficult, but doing so had a calming effect. The memory was really hazy, and then their visit, two actually, a week a part, became clear. They were only four years older than me. We had a lot in common. They even stopped one afternoon for a couple hours to play soccer with Raul and me at our school, but after that, I didn't see them again. They visited Mrs. Washburn, too. She said they were transferred to the west side of town. I tried to remember what they said about agency.

"It's the right to choose between right and wrong, or something like that."

"Yes, something like that. It is the power to think, choose, and act for ourselves. It is a universal law. Wherever you go in the universe, agency is there, so whenever a situation arises requiring people to make a choice, they have the right to do that. Let's say you need money to buy candy, but the piggy bank is empty. You have a choice. Wait for your allowance, find work to earn it, or get into your grandmother's purse and steal it."

"I'd never steal from Grandma."

The captain held up a hand as a polite way to tell me to shut up and listen.

"You have a choice. Now, Lucifer will encourage you to steal the money. It's fast, easy, and who would know?"

"Grandma. She knows to the penny how much is in her purse." Sometimes I can be a slow learner about taking instructions. He tilted his head down and slightly to the right as if looking over a pair of glasses, just like Aunt Florence and Grandma. "Sorry. I'll shut up."

"And what would happen if you did steal some money from your grandmother?"

"She would be very disappointed and hurt, and I'd get one heck of a lecture about honesty, not to mention probably not seeing daylight for a month."

"Consequences. You see, we have the right to make choices, but with every choice you make there are consequences attached. Some good, some bad. And those consequences do not always effect you only. Now, Señor Vasquez, your grandmother, or me would have told you this adventure of yours was foolhardy, dangerous . . ."

"You did. It was stupid."

"Let's say not well conceived, but you and Alejandro were set on doing it . . ."

"Come hell or high water."

"Yes. The best any of us could do was make suggestions. Whether you took those suggestions was entirely up to you, like when I pointed to this old farmstead. You could have ignored me and gone your merry way, whatever direction it might have been."

"But we didn't even know about the place."

"That's correct. That is a way we can work from this side of life – provide knowledge of options. Again, whether you listen or not is your right.

"Now, regarding this action, granted, it was based on something I once did, but would there have been any way to dissuade you from the path you chose to take? Your love for Concepción is too great to be tempered by reason. Perhaps it is a family trait, but you let your emotions rule judgment. I can only provide what little assistance I can, Francis. I can not intervene with any consequence of your choices. In this matter, whether you live or die is in your hands."

"And whether the others live or die falls on me, too," I answered, feeling the hopelessness of our situation. "And I charged right into this thing like it was some great James Bond movie. I not only jeopardized their lives, but their chances to get into Heaven because they killed some of those men today."

"You haven't been reading your Bible, have you?"

"What do you mean?"

"Remember when Abraham's nephew, Lot, decided to live in Gomorrah? The city revolted and was overrun by an army lead by Chedorlaomer, King of Elam."

"I remember Gomorrah getting destroyed by God."

"The same place, but that happened later, and that and the willingness to sacrifice his son is about all people remember about that time in Abraham's life. When Sodom, Gomorrah, and three other cities refused to pay their taxes and revolted, King Chedorlaomer attacked them. When he captured Gomorrah, they took Lot captive. Abraham led an army of 318 to rescue his nephew. Quite the military strategists, that man, to defeat a huge army with only 318 soldiers, but that aside, do you think no one was hurt or killed?

"And Moses. He killed an Egyptian, and Joshua led the army of Israel to clean out the land promised to them. Do you suppose there were no deaths then? And King David with Goliath? I could go on, but the point is that the war against evil often involves death. That does not necessarily preclude a person from returning to God's presence."

"But, what about you?"

"True, I was defending my family and others from the aggression of evil, but I need not have let my emotions rule judgment. I need not have done what I did. They were willing to surrender. I yielded to my emotions and hundreds died needlessly."

"So we could die tomorrow."

"Someone always dies tomorrow, Francis," he answered soberly.

The silence that followed allowed me to reflect on a very gloomy realization. Not that I might be denied Heaven, but that I might be getting there a little sooner than expected, or worst still, being the impetus for people I love getting there sooner than they should. He left when Franz came to relieve me.

Sitting where the Captain had been, he obviously wanted to speak, just not sure how to start. Hesitating to give him some time, he finally broke the silence as I was about to leave.

"I did not want this to go unsaid. I am grateful what you have done für me today."

"I may have only prolonged the inevitable," I said sadly.

"But at least this way I have chance to die mit dignity."

"You would have done that back in the cave. I'm sorry, but all my stupid, fantasizing heroics only extended your suffering."

"It nicht stupid heroics, David Evreux. Sie haben mir chance zu leben." Franz was becoming very passionate as his English began to fail. After a brief pause to compose, he translated, "You have given ein chance to live. If I must die, at least I can do as true German, fighting, *nicht als eine dumme Kuh zu schlachten genommen* . . . not as a stupid cow taken to slaughter."

I sat back down, humbled by his bravery. I wanted to know more about such a person.

"You don't have to answer, but . . . but what makes a guy . . well . . .?

"Attracted to men rather than women?"

"Yeah."

"That ist fair question. I do not know, David. I ask myself that many times. It ist big struggle to understand. I do not dislike women. They can be enjoyable to be around. We can talk of many things—music, clothes, books, celebrities--but they just do not hold der same physical attraction as they do for you. Doctors have many theories. Some say such ist a chemical imbalance. Some say such ist hereditary, dictated by der person's genetics. That greatly disturbs der man who fathered me. He is afraid my being gay reflects upon him. He argues like many, that such ist a matter of choice." I detected a rising bitterness in his voice when speaking of his father.

"It must be a hard life in the world we live."

"Hard? To live in world mit so much intolerance, ignorance, und lack of compassion für how such as I feel and hurt? Ja, ist hard, but in some ways ist becoming better, slowly."

"So what will you do, if we get out of this mess?"

There was silence before he answered. "I think I will do what ist expected of any person, make a way through this life best I can. In that journey, I would like to attend a university, und then travel der world in search of answers to questions that have plagued mankind für many thousands of years. What about you?"

"Well, ever since last year, I've become fascinated with archeology."

"Concepción said you discovered great pirate's treasure."

"It belonged to my ancestor. I haven't told anyone, not even Alejandro and Concepción, but there's more, a lot more, a whole lot more, scattered throughout the Caribbean Ocean. I want to find them. It's not for money. I have plenty, but according to my ancestor's journal they contain artifacts from civilizations Spain in particular tried to totally destroy. They may answer questions about things we have had no answers to.

"A worthy career. I envy you."

"It may not be as easy as it sounds. I know where they are located, but someone else may know, too. They want the treasures purely for the money. It may not be any safer a pursuit than what we face right now."

"You would be like Indiana Jones."

I chuckled. "Yeah. Now that you mention it."

"When we are free of this, I will buy you a whip . . . as soon as I earn enough money."

We both laughed, but the way he said when, not if, I felt a kind of strength enter my body.

Chapter 14

Taking the Offensive

As the first morning light brought our shelter out of physical darkness, our little group huddled together contemplating a dreary future.

"Okay, enough of this," I said, shattering the oppressive silence. "If we are going to live through this, we need to stop digging mental holes in which to bury ourselves. Leaving here puts us out in the open. All they'd have to do then is stand out of range or fly overhead and shoot us down."

"We can't stay here much longer without food," Alejandro said.

"No, and I don't think we'll have to. After what we've done, they're going to send everything they've got after us. That probably means another helicopter, and that means they will spot the cars we wrecked. It's a no brainier we couldn't get far from there on foot. Then they will spot this place."

"They'll send men here," Concepción said.

"Exactly. Men in cars. If we're lucky, one."

"That means a shootout, you know," Alejandro protested.

"Yes, but there is only one approach into this place. We decide the terms on which the battle is to be waged."

"That means killing some or all of them," Concepción said.

"Well, it is not like we haven't already done that," Alejandro reminded her.

"I was reminded about the battle Abraham with King Chedorlaomer."

"Who?" Alejandro asked.

"He was the King of Elam. He attacked the city of Gomorrah and took Abraham's nephew, Lot, captive along with a lot of other people and treasure. Abraham gathered up men and went after them to rescue his nephew. He had a little over 300 armed men against a big army. He defeated them using strategy. The Dolphin took on forts and warships and won by using strategy. Well, we are about to take on an army, but it will be on our terms. We may win, we may not, but like Franz said to me last night, we can at least die with dignity, not like animals taken to slaughter."

For the next half hour Alejandro and I scouted the abandoned farmstead from the perspective of defense while Franz kept sentry on a knoll northeast of the ruins. There was only one-way in with a vehicle, along an almost invisible, rough, two-track trail. The only really suitable place to land a helicopter was about fifty yards in front of the house and barn. Our wait wasn't long before hearing the unmistakable beating sound of helicopter rotors reverberate across the rolling plain.

After lowering Lauro into a shallow hole toward the rear of the house I said, "Lauro, do not come out unless it is one of us. If this does not go our way, stay hidden until the bad men are gone, and then head for that flock of sheep. Hopefully, there will be someone tending them. Ask for their help." He looked up at me with incredibly expressive, large eyes. The fear and despondency were gone, replaced by what could only be hope and gratitude. "While you are down there, you might say a prayer or two that we make it." For the first time, a faint smile spread his lips as his head nodded, yes. Nothing could have given me more hope and determination.

Placing boards and some dirt over the top did a good job to conceal his location. I then grabbed a share of the guns and ammo and headed for the barn, slipping beneath broken, rotted boards. I didn't even want to think about what might be crawling around in there. Alejandro and Concepción took positions on either end of the rectangular ruins, hidden among bushes trying to devour the place. Franz hunkered down in a thick clump of stunted trees in a small wash not far from where a helicopter would land. In a shootout, the bad guys would have no cover except their vehicle. The one thing we did not want to do was to damage any they drove in.

As expected, the helicopter circled over the crash site. By the sounds, it landed. Of course, they would check out the wrecks to see if we were there. Ten minutes later the engines revved up. Lifting back into sight, it hovered a bit, and then flew to where we were hiding and circled several times. It then hovered, apparently looking for a decent landing site and wait for their ground forces to move in. They couldn't see us, but would have to check it out. My hands quivered.

Whenever the Dolphin attacked another ship, he refused the conventional method of battle. Instead of running parallel, he canted the cannon forward and approached at an angle making it easy to turn either way to bring either side of the Raven's guns to bear more quickly. Those first salvos were important. It was important to disable the opponent's ability to maneuver by rendering their sails incapable of holding the wind, or better still, de-mast them. Each of us understood that our first salvo had to be effective.

Presently, a black SUV pickup edged over the hill, creeping along the rutted trail. As it neared the flat, bare area in front of the house, the helicopter landed. I could see the pilot remain in the cockpit, the rotors rotating slowly. Two men jumped from the chopper and ran down the incline to join four men exiting the SUV, using it as a shield in case we were hiding in the ruins and began shooting. They were looking closely at the house using binoculars.

We waited.

I was surprised they hadn't made a move to check out the place, until spotting a second SUV inch over the hill, pulling up behind the first. As it neared, two men began walking, each heading toward the opposite ends of what once had been a house. A third moved toward my position. We waited. The three were half way to our positions as the second SUV pulled up and four men, two on each side, got out, looking around. Still, we waited. And then the wait was over.

The tat-tat-tat-tat from Franz's machine gun was the signal. The men wheeled around to face the direction from which they heard the shots. Just as the pilot leaped from the helicopter, it erupted into a black and orange fireball ejecting a shower of shrapnel. We opened fire. The first three coming toward us dropped instantly. Volleys from Alejandro and Concepción struck the two standing on the house side of the second SUV as well. I laid down fire on the guys standing on the chopper side of the vehicles. I hit one who spun around and ricocheted off the vehicle. The last four flattened on the ground to return fire, but only knew the general direction of the attack and didn't have any cover except from the shooters in the house. That's when Franz crawled out of hiding. He had a clear shot from an elevated position behind the burning chopper.

Once the guys on their side of the vehicle had been taken out, Alejandro and Concepción couldn't shoot because the vehicles were between them and the remaining gangsters, but Franz and I could. The firefight only last a few minutes, but it felt like an eternity. As quickly as it started, one of them raised one arm and shouted, "Arrendo! Arrendo! Non sparate! Arrendo!"

Fearing it could be a trick, I took careful aim best I could as Alejandro came out from the house and circled behind the truck, pointing his pistol at the man. When he waived, I wiggled out and moved toward him. Franz held his ground to cover us.

Concepción came forward, checking bodies, and kicking weapons away. Each of us was ready to shoot if any one of them decided to resurrect. I did the same as Concepción, but those encountered as I moved forward were no threat. The lone survivor had a wound in the thigh. He was lucky. While giving the all clear sign to Franz, Concepción quickly applied a pressure bandage to the man's wound and tied it off. We then laid him in the shade of the first SUV. Alejandro assumed the wheel of the second SUV as Franz and I flatted the other vehicle's tires and disabled the radio. Once Concepción retrieved Lauro, we piled into the vehicle, another four-door pickup. A few minutes later, we regained the spaghetti road and I consulted the map. That wasn't really necessary as I had it memorized by now, but seemed to be the thing to do.

The better part of a half hour passed tension at peak levels as we each nervously scanned the air for another chopper, and the road ahead and behind for cars, or dust which would indicate a vehicle coming our way. We knew more gangsters were out there with no idea if the chopper pilot had time to radio our position. Their appearance was sudden and unexpected, to them and us, as Alejandro was in the process of making a right turn around a bend in the road. Driving a little faster than he should have, our vehicle swung wide.

Half way through the turn another SUV appeared heading straight toward us. Alejandro swerved right, driving partially up the embankment. The encountering vehicle reflexively swung right into a ditch and stalled. Alejandro floored the accelerator launching us around the curve and out of sight. It wasn't long before they managed to get unstuck and offer pursuit, joined by another vehicle, which must have been some distance behind us.

Apparently, these guys were well aware of what we had done over the course of twenty-four hours and hung back, just out of effective shooting range – for either of us. That gave me the sinking feeling of being herded, not pursued.

"Stay alert. They're staying back for a reason," I said. Paranoia can be a good thing if not let to cripple one's thinking.

Coming on another relatively long, straight stretch of road over more gently undulating hills, Alejandro floored it again. I had no desire to look at the speedometer, knowing things were going passed at an awfully fast rate. That's when the lead car made its move to close the gap.

Rearmed with automatic rifles and lots of ammo, Concepción and Franz took aim, ready to squeeze off a few rounds as we crested a small swell when Alejandro cried out, "Oh, no!"

Just ahead the dirt road suddenly ended at a T-intersection. Our pursuers had indeed been herding us. Obviously their intention was to make us over drive and either miss the turn or better still, flip over.

"Right!" I yelled as his braking threw dirt and gravel in a great arching cloud, the back end doing a very nice job trying to take over the lead.

Bouncing onto a narrow, two-lane asphalt road the tires complained loudly. Everyone was sure we'd tip and roll into the pasture beyond like one of those beach balls with an off-set weight inside to make it fly in erratic ways. The vehicle leaned precariously, but remained upright as we slid enough sideways to be lined up for a squealing departure. Blinded by our dust, the pursuing vehicle apparently mis-judged the intersection as well, shot across the road, through the warning sign, and into a meadow. The bumps were now smoother, but I swear the road became more twisty than melting, plastic string. The second land rover easily negotiated the turn and began gaining on us.

"Oh, no!" Alejandro cried out again as our vehicle suddenly careened left then right.

"Stop saying that," I yelled.

My attention had been focused on the pursuing vehicle when Alejandro made that declaration; I turned enough to spot the problem – sheep standing on the shoulder of our portion of the road. He narrowly missed them, bringing to mind that first drive to Casa de St. Nazaire. The pursuing SUV swerved, too, but out too far. His left wheel caught the shoulder. Over-correcting, it shot off the right side of the road and plowed into a pile of rocks sending up a spray of plastic and rock fragments. He was out of the chase, but the SUV, which missed the intersection, had regained the road and was coming up fast. They must have had one heck of an engine.

"What side of the road should I drive on, left or right?" he asked.

"I don't know. Whatever side doesn't have cars coming at us," I answered.

"Road block!" Alejandro yelled after the fourth or fifth sharp turn. I lost count, concentrating on not getting carsick.

His incessant negativism by this time was really becoming annoying. However, this time he was re-ferring to an army-looking vehicle straddling the pavement's edge on our side. At least it was facing in the same direction we were rocketing.

"Go around!" I shouted.

Swerving, we streaked passed. The four men standing by the vehicle appeared to be wearing some kind of uniform, but we weren't of a mind to slow down and check it out. They were waving. We politely waved back as a couple leaped for the rela-tive safety of the adjacent pasture.

"Now we have two of them following us. That truck you passed is behind the gangsters," Concep-ción said. "Hey, it looks like they are shooting at each other. Perhaps I can help." Taking careful aim, she unleashed a short burst from the machine gun. Its tires punctured, the land rover swerved out of control and into the ditch, the following truck stopping right behind it.

Alejandro kept his foot pegged to the floorboards as we continued along the road, way too fast, as vineyards and olive orchards became a passing blur. Then more houses began to appear with more small herds of sheep and goats hazardously close to the road.

"Slow down. Slow down. We don't want to hit any of those, besides I think we're coming to a village," I said still trying to decipher the map and get better bearings.

He slowed. Sure enough, popping over a small hill we found ourselves coming to the outskirts of a village, and dead ahead a real roadblock of four, big army trucks, and lots of soldiers, everyone with a gun pointed at us. As we came to a squealing stop there was lots of yelling in Italian.

"Throw down your weapons! Put your hands on your heads! Do not move!" My Italian might have been lousy to non-existent, but it didn't take a scholar to understand what they wanted. Franz's translating helped. Out-gunned, we were certainly amenable to following instructions.

Swarming the vehicle, they ordered us out and line up along the road. "On your knees, hands behind your heads," one of them shouted, at least that's what Franz told us. We followed his lead.

Once our captors felt the situation under their

control, a short-barreled man with a big mustache tapped me on the shoulder with a riding crop and said, "Stare."

"He wants you to stand up," Franz said.

"Te, non parlare," he snapped at Franz, telling him to shut up, and popping his shoulder with the crop to emphasize the command.

"Lui non parla italiano." Franz was undaunted, telling him I did not speak Italian.

Taken off-guard a second, he wanted to know what language I did speak. "Quello che lingua parla?"

"Lui è americano. Parla inglese e spagnolo."

"You are American?" Mr. Mustache asked in thick English.

"Yes."

"My English is not so good. Do you understand?"

"It's a lot better than my Italian. Yes."

"I am Capt. Agapito Ponzio of the Corpo dei Carabinieri, Italian police," the man said. "I would like to know what is going on with all this crazy driving and shooting."

"Some of your Mafia dudes came to El Hierro where we live and kidnapped our sister. My brother and I came to rescue her."

Capt. Ponzio's stare at me was completely blank.

"Franz, you better tell him."

He started to explain in Italian, but Capt. Ponzio held up a hand to stop him. "I understand what you said. I just do not believe three boys could come into my country unnounced, go into the den of vipers, and rescue a girl. And what about the child?"

"Only me and my brother came. Franz, the tall one, and the child were also prisoners. We weren't going to leave them behind."

Ponzio remained silent, the flat of his hand on his head as it shook it slowly from side to side in disbelief. Finally he said to Franz in Italian, "qual è il tuo nome?"

Franz answered in English. "My name is Franz Galfridus."

"The son of the German banker who sent mercenaries to shoot up our countryside looking for you?"

"Yes."

Ponzio turned away to mutter something that didn't sound very polite, and then turned back. "Who is the child?"

"Lauro Guzzanti, . . ."

The captain loosed another epithet, much louder, and turned very pale. I thought he was going to faint.

"Please, stand up, and put your arms down. Please. Stand. I greatly appologize for your treatment in our country. Is there something I can get for you?"

"Some water would be nice," Concepción said.

Instantly, the captain snapped his fingers and shouted, "Acqua. Portare loro l'acqua." Turning back to us he asked, "Are you hungary as well?"

"Yes," Franz answered quickly. It had been a

long time since he had eaten anything and I wondered how he had done it.

"E razioni. Presto! Presto!" the captain shouted more emphatically.

The soldiers nearly stumbled over themselves to bring us water and share their rations.

"What you have done is a miracle. You are very lucky. Crazy, but lucky. How did you enter my country?"

Alejandro and I looked at one another, silently agreeing not mentioning anything about Capt. Santana.

"Let's just say, we dropped in?"

"I see. Did you bring weapons when you . . . dropped in?"

I hesitated. "How should I answer that, Captain?"

"No."

"No."

He smiled and cupped a hand behind my neck. "Che coraggio! What bravery."

A few minutes later the goons chasing us were brought in. There were only two and they looked as if they'd been through a carwash without the water.

"Can you show me where you found the hostages?" Ponzio said, spreading a much better map over the hood of his vehicle.

Locating Regio di Clabria, and then Sicia, I traced a finger north to the little coastal village. "About here. There is a fancy villa overlooking the village and marina."

"Ah, yes. I know of where you speak."

"We sort of borrowed a couple scooters and drove five miles north to . . .," my finger traced along the squiggly line. ". . . To here. This intersection." The finger kept moving another six miles. "The cave they are using is about here. When we started back the guards at this intersection blocked the road back to the village so we turned up this road. We have a map, not a very good one, but it gave us a general direction to go. It then just came down to evading the guys chasing us." When I mentioned the T-intersection and abandoned farm, he was able to locate the ruins for me.

"You will find a helicopter there, or what's left of it, and another vehicle. There are ten bodies there. One guy is wounded. We left him in some shade with water."

"Ten!"

"Off the road, here, you will find two more vehicles and five more bodies."

"Five! More?"

"And back this way, somewhere around here, you will find some more vehicles and possibly another helicopter. I don't know how many may have been injured or killed there."

"Santa Madre! Three boys, one girl, and a child have done all that!"

I shrugged. There was no time then, but thinking on it afterward, we did plow across the countryside leaving death and destruction in our wake like a German Panzer Division.

Capt. Ponzio really poured on the hospitality,

having a couple of wool blankets spread under the cool shade of a big tree, and some real food and fresh bread retrieved from the village as we waited for transportation that would start our journey home.

On the surface, I saw this as coming from a man with a kind heart, but over the past year, I developed a skepticism about adult intentions. I saw this generosity and concern as genuine, but also cloaking a way to get more information. Alejandro was on the same page as we often spoke to one another with our eyes, hedging answers that the captain really wanted.

As I said, Capt. Ponzio is a kind man with a large, and I do mean large, family. It took fifteen or twenty minutes, but Lauro relaxed enough to sit next to him and let him playfully ruff his hair. Knowing he was safe, he even gave a little laugh as they talked. Privately told what Lauro had endured and his silence, the captain knew not to revisit the nightmare and talked to him only about things that would interest little boys.

An hour later the beat of a helicopter echoed over the rolling pastures, joined by another. A nervous shiver visited my back upon hearing that sound until my brain overrode the ingrained fear reaction. The noise grew progressively louder until breaking over a line of olive trees. There was a large, two rotor one accompanied by a smaller, single rotor one. The big one hovered over the levelest part of the pasture, scattering sheep to a safe distance before landing. As it seemed to heave a sigh and rest on the ground, the second landed a bit further beyond.

"Your carriage awaits you, Señorita," Ponzio said to Concepción, extending a hand to help her stand. By the way she flashed an almost undetectable grimace indicated she was as stiff and sore and the rest of us. Lauro jumped up and latched onto her hand. The captain knelt by him and stroked his thick head of hair tenderly. "It is alright, little one. That great machine will take you to where your momma and papa will be able to come for you. You are such a brave boy. I have been honored to know you."

With the five of us safely buckled into the largest helicopter, it lifted from the outskirts of the normally quiet, little village, Capt. Ponzio with the great mustache waving farewell. I began to relax, and like Lauro, watch the landscape slip below as we flew to a military base at Cozenza where we could truly relax and begin to feel civilized again. At ground level, the tortured terrain was a blurred nightmare. From the air I could better appreciate the miracle we survived, a magnificent blend of green valleys rising at incredibly steep angles to grayish-white peaks scared by the most nightmarish, serpentine roads imaginable.

Chapter 15

The Mafioso and the Army

Passing over the mountain range, we could see the ocean off to our left. Somewhere a hundred miles behind us, Capt. Santana lay offshore – fishing. The land below was a mottled, emerald green patchwork of orchards and vineyards, dotted with white, stucco houses, and villages. Finally, more urbanized structures appeared as we approached our destination, a military base. Circling once, our helicopter zeroed in on a large, gold circle with a white cross in the middle. The pilot set us down exactly in the center as gently as handling a carton of eggs.

After the rotors stopped, the crew allowed us to deplane. An austere-looking woman, I guessed in her late twenties, light brown hair wrapped in a tight bun, and wearing the uniform of a lieutenant met us on the edge of the tarmac standing next to two shiny, white cars. Despite her outward appearance, Lt. Porrelli is a very caring person, not unlike Capt. Ponzio. Assigned to what could be described as the public relations branch of the military, she saw to our immediate needs, the first being a hot shower. However, that presented a problem.

Upon landing, Lauro retreated into his safe shell, once again clinging to Concepción as if his body was coated in Velcro. I had to agree. The military base was so stark to be a little frightening and secretly wished I could hold her hand, too. However, Lauro's actions became humorous. He refused to leave Concepción's side, which made for an interesting shower. He had become a little warmer with me, but it took a lot of coaxing to allow Sis out of his sight behind the shower curtain. I eventually had to sit outside her shower to keep him company until she reappeared wrapped in towels, one around her body, and one like a turban on her head. Then Lauro interjected another problem. He refused to shower until Concepción agreed to wait outside while he showered – with me. That was okay until the kid stuck his head around the curtain several times to be sure she was truly still there.

"Oh, for cryin' out loud, would you talk, or sing, or something so he knows you haven't left," I called out when he opened the curtain for a third time.

"What? Are you feeling self-conscious about showing too much?" she retorted.

By this point, I was beyond tired and cranky.

Instead of a smart retort, I was about to throw the curtain open and bare all, but my hand stopped just as I grabbed the material. Sis began singing. I'd never heard her sing. She had a beautiful voice. Obviously satisfied, Lauro looked up at me with those great big, brown eyes and smiled, a much bigger smile. If ever I had a justifiable excuse to prolong a shower, listening to her voice was enough. As the hot water cascaded over my body, muscles unwound and began to fully relax for the first time since leaving Marbello. That's when I heard the Captain's voice.

"Francis."

It was a whisper. Casting about through the cascading water and steam there was nothing to go with the voice.

"Don't bother looking. I don't want to upset the lad. Just listen. It is good to not mention Capt. Santana."

"Yes, sir. I thought so, too," I answered, causing Lauro to glance up at me.

Eventually turning off the water, Lauro hopped out into a towel Concepción held out. I was a lot more modest.

"Would you hand me a towel, please," I asked.

"Oh, are you still in there? It has been so long, I thought you melted and washed down the drain," she countered, passing a towel around the edge of the curtain.

"No. I was just enjoying hearing you sing."

There was total silence. As I stepped from the

shower, appropriately wrapped, she was kneeling next to a bundled Lauro, rubbing him dry. She looked up. There was no smile, no frown, no expression except in her eyes. What I saw is hard to explain. It was a moment, a feeling we both clung to until Alejandro broke onto the scene.

"So, did the three of you enjoy your shower together and leave any hot water?"

Concepción stood up quickly, turned her head so not to look at her brother, and shuffled Lauro out of the room. Alejandro watched her, confused. Then at me.

"You didn't . . .?"

"No, we did not. She's exhausted. Sis is a very strong woman, but the strain she's been under . . . I don't think we can really know how hard it was."

"Yeah, it's been hard . . . on all of us. Now it's over," he said, tossing his dirty clothes in a heap on the floor and stepping into the shower. "Ah-h-h, hot water."

"It's not quite over, Alejandro," I said over the sound of water and hedonistic moans.

"What do you mean, not quite over?"

"We still have to face Papa, Grandma, and Aunt Herminia."

There was a long silence as the water cascaded on. Finally, he said, "You didn't have to remind me," and then returning to his usual lightheartedness, "Oh, well. I'll live for the moment and enjoy, but it seems a shame to have come this far to die by the hands of family."

Attired in clean clothes graciously provided by the army quartermaster, we received a hot meal after which we spoke with Colonel Antonio D'Alema, the Base Commander. As it was necessary to make a report, he wanted to hear all about our adventure. Like Capt. Ponzio, he was particularly interested as to how Alejandro and I arrived on Italian soil. Again, we only vaguely referred to dropping in. He pressed the issue rather forcefully.

"This map you used, it is a smuggler's map. Did you know that?" he said.

"I suspected as much," I answered calmly.

"I must ask again, how did you enter our country?"

"Colonel D'Alema, we are deeply grateful for the intervention of your police and soldiers, and providing us with an opportunity to refresh ourselves, but for the sake of those who helped us, we must remain silent out of greater gratitude. I hope you can understand." Really too tired to come up with that particular wording, I was grateful the Captain stepped in at that moment as he did a year ago.

D'Alema stared at me and then at Alejandro, his dark eyes attempting to bore a confession from us. "If you will not reveal your accomplices, perhaps you will explain why you undertook such a positively crazy thing?"

"We love our sister," I fired back on my own. "Hey, we're teenagers. We live on impulse."

His head tilted forward into an open hand to

stare at his desk, but by the slight quaking of his shoulders, I knew he was strangling a laugh. He had teenage children. He knew.

Looking back at us, recomposed and appearing serious again, he continued, "You had no confidence that we would do everything possible to rescue your sister and the others?"

"Colonel, I'm just a kid. I am not smart in political things, so I am probably going to offend you, but you want the truth. How long have these kidnappings been going on? What have you done to rescue others?"

That threw him on the defensive. "We are preparing a campaign . . ."

"Preparing. As you would say, by the grace of God, my brother and I arrived seconds – literally seconds before they pulled the trigger and put a bullet in Franz's head. With all your preparations, he would not be alive today. Lauro's father would have given in, and who knows what they were demanding of him, and we would have paid their ransom and made them even richer. Our decision to come here was on pure impulse, but looking back, we would do it again."

I could see the colonel was upset. Holding a clenched fist at his mouth, his dark eyes glared at us, and then his anger softened as a slight smile appeared beneath his thick, salt and pepper mustache. I knew then he understood.

"You are the first ever to escape captivity from the Mafioso stronghold. That it was accomplished by children is absolutely amazing. They will certainly be the subject of much laughter instead of fear for some time to come. I can only hope a few of my soldiers will show the bravery you have demonstrated, foolish and stupid as it was. What you did was magnificent."

Chapter 16

CIC Takes the Boot

Late that afternoon Col. D'Alema called us back to his office. The Spanish and German Consulates were there so we could call our families and make arrangements to be reunited. Papa Vasquez and Grandma were still in Marbello where we reached them on their cell phone. They insisted we each speak to them as reassurance we were well. Franz initially spoke with his mother, but it was obvious when his father came on the phone. He was not at all pleased with his father for refusing to pay the ransom and getting him within a trigger's pull of death. I don't speak German, but by the tone of his voice, Franz said some pretty acrimonious things.

That evening we gathered in the dormitory

lounge, Concepción and I on a sofa with Lauro curled between us, his head on her lap. Alejandro and Franz sat in loungers, the German with legs folded under him, my brother typically draped over the arms. After what we experienced, a special bond had formed and Franz obviously felt comfortable speaking about personal things.

"I have been very reluctant to tell anyone I am gay. Finding someone who is not judgmental as you is very difficult," he said.

I never thought about that. Me not making judgments about other people. Without realizing it, I didn't until after knowing them and learning what kind of person they really were. It was like with Raul. When he first came to our school, I didn't notice that his skin color was different. His accent didn't bother me, either. I thought it was cool and even attempted to imitate it. We became close friends because I liked something about him that went beyond the superficial. Now, Fuentes was different. An instant dislike boiled up because of how he acted toward other people. As for Franz, well, he was just another guy. Very likable. His sexual orientation was a non-issue as far as I was concerned.

"When I war fifteen they caught another boy and I kissing in closet at school."

"Is that when you came out?" I could feel Concepción's elbow about to launch into my ribs.

Franz looked at me a moment, obviously trying to translate my sick joke, and then suddenly clapped his hands and laughed. "Yes! That ist the time I came out of meine closet. Very goot, David."

Concepción held short puncturing my lung, but kept that weapon ready.

"When I come out of closet, I sit mit counselor at school. He war der first person I tell of meine feelings toward other boys. He understood und encouraged me to at least inform meine parents. Miene vater threatened to disown me and sent me to military school to get meine head fixed right. There were others at der school like me. Vater did not know the schoolmaster was gay, also." He chuckled. "We learn how to live in der world der way we are, not be shaped by others. Meine vater only sent those men to appease meine mutter. I would not be surprised they should kill me if they had been able."

"What will you do?" Concepción asked.

"I have uncle on meine mutter's side. I can stay mit him."

"Is your uncle going to accept your choice of lifestyle?" Concepción asked.

"He does not agree mit meine beliefs. He has always been kind man, und let me to stay at his house when meine vatter and I have big arguments. I will tell der newspapers meine story. I will tell them about der man who was . . . how do you say it in America? . . . ein samenspender . . . sperm donor."

I thought both Alejandro and Concepción were going to choke. I had to laugh. Just the way he pulled that off was a precious moment. Too bad his father couldn't hear that then, although the man heard that description more than a few times later. In fact, Franz refused to call him father, instead addressing him as Herr Samenspender.

"Meine uncle lives in Strasbourg. That is one hour south from Frankfurt where meine mutter lives. I am not known there. I will find work and earn enough money to attend school. There are many universities in Germany."

"What do you wish to study?" Concepción asked.

"I would like to study Anthropology, the study of man."

Now, it was my turn to laugh. Their quizzical looks nearly broke me up completely, but I was un-daunted as my strange sense of humor rose to the surface, "Seems appropriate, the study of man."

Concepción scowled and was about to upbraid the remark with her elbow when Franz came right back.

"And you are interested in Archaeology, the sci-ence of digging?"

We looked at each other, the twinkle in my mis-chievous eyes reflected in his. For once! Somebody with my sense of humor! We both broke into broad smiles and laughter, launching a long friendship.

We continued talking into the early morning hours. Concepción and Franz feeling better to relate the story of their ordeals, and Alejandro and I about coming to Italy, sans a few small details like exactly how we arrived and who helped us, just in case the room was bugged. Lauro continued to remain pain-fully silent, curled between us, eventually falling sound asleep – the first truly safe rest he had been privileged for many weeks.

Eventually, I could see Concepción was about to

crash as well. Gently cradling the petite child in my arms, I carried him to Sis's room and looked around, undecided on which cot to lay him.

Stepping into the room, she pointed to a bed, only slightly wider than a cot. "He can sleep with me. That's what he did in the cave."

Laying him down, I turned. She was staring at me. "What?" I said.

"You're going to make a great father someday," she said, and then taking both my hands into hers, she raised up on her toes and kissed my cheek.

Walking down the corridor to my quarters, I pictured her cradling him in a reassuring hug. The little boy in me would have liked something like that on at least one occasion, too, but the dominoes never fell in such a way to provide that very special comfort.

In our room, Alejandro had dropped onto his cot fully clothed and was well under way at snoring his way through the remainder of the night. Franz was back to his underwear and sliding beneath the sheets. Sleep came quickly until sitting bolt upright in bed sometime during the pre-dawn morning hour.

"Something wrong?" a familiar voice asked softly. The Captain was seated in a chair near the foot of my cot reading a book.

"Capt. Santana! He's waiting to pick us up just off the coast."

"Oh, he knows all that happened. He listened to everything on the radio, both the gangsters and the military. He is well equipped for his avocation. When he heard you were safe, he said a prayer and returned to Spain. That's good, Francis. You got someone to say a prayer. That will help right some of your behavior."

"My behavior?" Then a chill slithered down my back. In my zeal to help Concepción I had violated, no, more like shattered more than a few of God's laws. I slumped back onto the bed, the concern for mortal survival replaced by concern for any life later. I had definitely scored a black mark or two . . . or three . . . in St. Peter's book.

"Relax. It's not all that serious. You are still alive, the best condition in which one can repent."

"But I don't belong to any church. I don't like them," I replied, sitting up.

"Yes, I know," he said with a sigh. "But you will learn differently . . . in time. Meanwhile, you can pray and seek forgiveness on your own."

"Pray?"

"Do you believe in God?"

"Well, yes."

"That's a good start. When is the last time you prayed?"

I had to think. "Grandma took me to church the Sunday before we left for El Hierro. The minister said a prayer."

"That doesn't count. When have *you* prayed?"

I thought back upon my life – way back. "When my dad was alive he came to tuck me in for the night. We would kneel together by the bed and he would pray. I guess he was teaching me how to do that . . . before he got killed."

"It is very simple, actually. You kneel next to your bed and talk to God as if you are talking to me or anyone else. Tell him what you did, and if you did anything wrong that you are sorry. Of course, you must mean that."

"Like killing those gangsters?"

"Yes, for starters."

"There's more?"

"A few, but I do not have enough fingers and toes to keep track."

I fell back onto the pillow.

He laughed. "Do not worry about everything at once. Start with . . . as you say, the big stuff."

"Killing all those men. I am not really sorry for that. They were the evil you told me about and they would have killed any of us without so much as second thought. I'd do it again in a heartbeat. "

"Yes, you would," the Captain said with a slight smile. "As I said the other night, there are times such things are justified. It was not heartless murder driven by uncontrolled passion."

"The French warship attacking Valverde," I said, remembering how he attacked the crippled ship and sunk it.

The Captain sighed. "Yes, that. Many, too many died needlessly because I lost control of my emotions. Unfortunately, there were others, as you shall learn. The important thing to remember from my experiences, Francis, is to always, always be in control of your emotions. Never allow them to control you. And pray for forgiveness while you are alive. Repentance is very hard once you are dead."

With those words ringing in my mind, he closed the book and was gone, leaving me to restlessly ponder that conversation. A flicker of light began filtering through the small window when I furtively slipped out of bed to kneel on the floor. Other than sit on a pew or at the dinner table, I didn't know how to really do that prayer stuff the Captain spoke about, but mimicked what my dad had started to teach me.

I don't know if the wording was proper, but following the Captain's suggestion, I imagined speaking to God as if He were on the other end of a telephone. I did end with "Amen," before climbing back into bed, feeling more at ease.

Late that morning, we had the dining hall pretty much to ourselves when a well-dressed man and woman entered, Lt. Porrelli at their side. Our petite charge was busily stuffing a third bowl of cereal down when I tapped his forearm and pointed toward the door.

With a high-pitched squeal of "Papa! Momma!" he leaped up, overturning the nearly empty bowl and nearly the long table as well. Even the others swear his bare feet only touched the tile floor two or three times before leaping into Señor Guzzanti's arms.

There were lots of tear, even from us, as the reunion unfolded. Then the boy who said nothing became as vocal as a politician on the campaign trail, jabbering excitedly, and pointing toward us. Taking their hands, he all but dragged the weeping parents to our table.

"Señorita, señors, grazie, grazie," was all the gentleman could say as his round face screwed up as a great river of tears flowed down puffy, olive-brown cheeks.

Concepción, the one who knows how things should be, rose, and let him wrap her into a big hug. After a few minutes, he held her at arm's length a moment before leaning forward to kiss her forehead. She then embraced Lauro's mother who had been standing silently in her husband's shadow. In turn, he kissed the three of us on both cheeks, a first for me. We then received a similar kiss from Señora Guzzanti. That was more comfortable.

From that time, there was a silence, but each knew what was in the heart of the other as grateful parents held their son's hands tightly, finally turning to leave. However, as they reached the door, Lauro broke free of their grip and sprinted back into Concepción's arms to squeeze off a hug. Looking up with those big, brown eyes and displaying a big, toothy grin, he said, "Thank you," in very good English, and was gone.

Each of us sat in silence allowing the last vestiges of Lauro's joyous squeals to fade from our mind's ears. Conversation resumed, but it was intermittent. Franz told how it was to live in Germany, Alejandro about El Hierro, me about America. Surprisingly, we did a lot of the same things as kids. Concepción remained silent.

Papa Vasquez and Grandma arrived by chartered jet just before noon. Likewise, there was a great round of hugs, and then some pretty stern lectures started until I held up a hand.

"Stop. You do not understand how much we love each other," I said, "especially the love Alejandro and I have for Concepción. We would gladly die for her."

"Except by the grace of God you nearly did!" Papa interrupted.

"You're wasting your breathe. We would do it again, and if it be God's will we die, we shall do so knowing we did what was right," Alejandro fired back.

Our position was plain. There would be no more argument or lectures.

"Alright," Grandma conceded, but I knew she wouldn't let the subject drop entirely. "We do have another little problem. The news people got wind of what happened. The paparazzi found out which hotel we were staying at in Marabella. There are reporters hanging around the entrance to the base and they saw us arrive. We spoke to that nice Colonel. He says they will expect a statement about what happened. His people are working on that, and we need to coordinate with them before saying anything. It will be necessary to smooth over some embarrassment you've caused the government. Getting into the country, shooting . . . oh, my God, Francis, shooting all those men!"

"I'm not a mass murderer, Grandma. It was self-defense."

"I know, I know, but still. They've recovered seventeen bodies so far and still counting, not to mention those who were injured. And you shot down two helicopters!"

"Wow! We did some serious hurt, brother!" Alejandro piped in. Concepción cut short further comments when she nailed his rib with the elbow. The fierce scowls from Papa and Grandma added to a quick dive for obscurity.

"We need to discuss what to say for now."

"We need to let people know what kind of scumbags we had to deal with, too."

"I agree, Francis, but perhaps those details would be better done later."

"Another book?"

"Hey, I have a great title," Alejandro piped up. He never could keep his head down for very long. "The Canary Island Commandos Take the Boot."

"Perhaps an even better title would be The Canary Island Commandos Receive the Boot," Papa suggested. For some reason, that released the mounting tension as we all laughed. In any event, that was the birth of the CIC, which would become an important part of our lives.

About then, Lt. Porrelli walked into the mess hall accompanied by another man and headed directly toward us. Capt. Tiziano was her superior. For the next hour, we discussed a statement to the press. My suggestion was a reversal of earlier feelings and took everyone by surprise.

Chapter 17

An Italian Holiday

Capt. Tiziano stepped to a battery of micro-phones set up outside the base's main gate. Clearing his throat to shut down their buzzing conversation, he began. "Signore e signori della stampa, ladies and gentlemen of the press, good day. I am Capt. Lorenzo Tiziano, Public Information Officer for the 91st Infantry Regiment Lucania. At my right is our commanding officer, Col. Antonio D'Alema.

"Several days ago, the combined forces of the 91st Infantry Regiment Lucania and 11th Carabinieri Battalion "Puglia" in Bari launched a mission against the De Stefano Mafioso family. We here to address that operation. A printed release with a few more details will be available at the conclusion of this news conference. Col. D'Alema wants you to know that no more information will be released at this time until the on-going operation is complete to protect those who are still in the field of battle."

"Several weeks ago, members of the De Stefano family kidnapped the daughter of a wealthy Spanish family and transported her to their hideout in the Aspromonte mountains near their nest outside of Sicia. She was only the most recent of a number such children to be afflicted with such debasing treatment. Yes, we have been aware of these atrocities, however we had no intelligence as to where they were being held.

"A major break in the case occurred when one of their number was left behind and taken into custody by a private security force. Let me say immediately, that neither the police of Spain or our country were involved in the initial interrogation, however the person captured divulged information that was vital to preparing our operation. This information immediately led to the arrest of Raffaele De Steffano, a boss within the 'Ndrangheta de Calabria by Spanish authorities before he could leave their jurisdiction. Spain will prosecute Raffaele De Steffano for his crimes. Additional information from him led us to know exactly where to find the young señorita.

Having this intelligence, a secret commando unit raided the place the señorita was being held and freed her as well as two other prisoners. The parents of these captives have requested that we not divulge their names at this time to avoid further traumatizing. I can assure you that all of the children are in good, physical condition.

"I might add, that during the commando operation, Giovanni, younger brother of Raffaele, was injured at the place where the children were held. He has been located and placed in custody. There have been no injuries to any of the commando unit or to our military and police forces. There were substantial casualties inflicted upon the De Stefano family.

"While the victims and their families do not wish to make a public appearance, they have asked me to read a statement."

Don't think that didn't rattle the newsies. As Capt. Tiziano began to read, Col. D'Alema stood stoically at his elbow, but you just knew the buttons on his uniform were put to the test with all the glowing things we had to say about the "intervention" and help provided by the Italian police and Army.

"Printed copies of this statement will also be available when I finish along with the other information. As I said earlier, this is an on-going operation; therefore, there will be no questions when I am through. I repeat, we will answer no questions. The following statement is prepared by the families of the children who were rescued.

"We wish to express our sincere gratitude to President of the Italian Republic, Giorgio Napolitano, the officers and staff of the Italian Supreme Defense Council, the Comando delle Forze Operative Terrestri, the Infantry Division Command Acqui *in San Giorgio a Cremano and members of the 2nd Army Aviation Regiment Sirio at Lamezia Terme. Specifically, we wish to extend our gratitude to Colonel Antonio D'Alema, Commander of the 91st Infantry Regiment Lucania here in Potenza, and to Capt. Agapito Ponzio of the Corpo dei Carabinieri, 11th Carabinieri Battalion "Puglia" in Bari, and to their officers and men for the rescue of our loved ones from the clutches of local gangsters. Our children are safe and well. We are returning home, but do so with much love and affection for all the kindness extended to us during a very trying time by the people, government officials of Italy, and these fine, brave soldiers and police officers."*

After reading the release in Italian, the reporters began screaming questions immediately. They don't listen to directions any better than I do.

"Where are the children? Can we talk to them? Can we get pictures of the children? Was one of the captives the son of a German banker? What about Señor Guzzanti's son? Was he with them?" To this Capt. Tiziano raised a hand for silence.

"All the captives are now in the safe arms of family and have returned to their homes. If they wish to grant interviews or stand for photographs, they will contact the news agencies. As I have stated previously, for security reasons there will no further comment on this continuing operation. That is all. Thank you."

Amid continued cries for more information the two officers left, Col. D'Alema sporting a faint, satisfied smile beneath his bushy mustache. Grandma had crafted much of the statement to remove any embarrassment and provide the military and police with credit. It also paved the way for us to secretly leave and blend back into the populace in peace, at least until such time we released the truth.

Behind a building, out of sight of the news people, Col. D'Alema joined us for the walk back to the barracks. The Spanish Consulate attaché followed just behind next to the information people. Hands behind his back, he said, "And what are your plans now?"

"Well, since we are already here, I for one would like to see a little more of Italy, as a tourist. My brother's driving didn't allow for a lot of sightseeing," I piped up.

"After all this, a real holiday would be nice," Grandma added.

"If you would like, I can arrange a tour of the country," the attaché said.

"No offense, but I'd like to pick up some clothes and return these to Col. D'Alema," Concepción said.

He surprised us all with a big, rolling laugh. "I totally agree. They, as both my teenage daughters would say, they are not you. I know just the places for you to go. Heaven knows I have spent a substantial amount of money there," he said. "Capt. Tiziano can provide the necessary transportation, and then I would be very honored to have you as my guests for diner this evening in my home."

Grandma and Concepción delightedly took off on their first-ever shopping trip together alone, guided by the señorita attaché and Lt. Porelli. Us guys struck out with Capt. Tiziano who proved adroit in avoiding the swarming camera fiends hovering around the base entrances. He also knew the clothiers in Cozenza the colonel mentioned, and the best places to eat.

Since divorcing himself from his father and refusing anything connected with the man, Franz was penniless. To prevent him from reverting to wearing a towel again we dragged him along and saw that he was properly attired. He definitely had a stodgy, conservative German bent as he browsed the dress slacks and polo shirt displays. Well, Alejandro and I knew that wouldn't do.

"Okay, Herr Franz. You're setting out on a new life. Time to loosen up and enjoy it," I scolded him in a light-hearted way. Alejandro and I taking each arm, we re-directed him to a much better selection.

Standing in front of the displays, there was a long silence as he looked first at Alejandro and then me before breaking into a big smile. "Ja. You are right. Life ist very delicate thing easily lost. Not often one gets der opportunity to begin fresh und folgen seinem Herzen . . . and follow his heart."

So much for dress slacks and polo shirts. He looked pretty touristy in sandals, shorts, and flowered shirts, and wouldn't feel out of place cruising with Alejandro and me except for the nearly pearly white legs. Of course we needed everything from top to bottom and inside out, and suitcases to stash it all in. Papa Vasquez prudently suggested we at least have some more formal attire, just in case. He was right, of course, so we added dress slacks, pastel colored shirts with statement ties, and a sports coat into the mix.

Franz's concern about the escalating costs were put at ease when I quietly said to him as we stepped into a private area to try our selections on. "Don't worry about the money. I literally have gobs and I really don't see any fun letting some banker get his fingers on it." Once again I let my mouth run off uncontrolled and looked at Franz rather panicked.

"You are totally correct, David. It ist your money. Enjoy while it lasts, and by der sounds of what you said before, there ist lot more than you already have."

As we walked out of the last clothier, I felt nearly blinded by his white legs. Again taking his arm, we J-walked to a tanning shop across the street. The young girl attending the reception area was quite attractive. Okay, she was a knock-out, and I more than envied Franz as the two disappeared into a small room. Twenty minutes later the German appeared with a better tan than mine!

"What'd she do?" I asked as we drove back to the base.

"First, I removed all my clothes, and then she applied some gel to my skin, rubbing it in very thoroughly."

"All!" Alejandro said. "Oh, my tan is getting awfully pale. I think I need some of that. Can we go back?"

"If you get any darker, you will look like one of those African gorillas," Papa said as I wondered if our two votes for going back outweighed his.

"It will not last long. Perhaps five or six days, but she gave some of these pills." I looked at the bottle, which of course had to be written in Italian.

"That would be beta-carotene, a healthy way to darken the skin without being sunburned," Papa said. "Especially for north Europeans. I don't think it would work very well for you two. Maybe turn you more orange."

As for our trip through Italy proper, the attaché personally arrange a private escort from the Italian Ministry of Tourism, but a week is little time to see such a varied country. The best we could do were whirlwind visits through Naples and Rome where dignitaries wined and dined us as well. A motor tour through the northern mountains was amazingly beautiful. We were not the children rescued by the Police and Army, but the Marqués Evreux and all that. The fun part was continually being a step ahead of the paparazzi who wanted me worst than the Mafioso. I think what threw them off was the fact we appeared so touristy. Even Papa relaxed with more casual attire, even to wearing Bermuda shorts. It was glorious and exhausting, and about to end when the evening before our planned last, full day which happened to be in Genoa, a formal invitation was received from Señor Guzzanti.

Reunited with Lauro, the Guzzanti family retired to their villa near Savona west of Genoa. He asked us to come and spend a couple days with them. The next morning a stretch limo pulled up to the hotel entrance. From there, we were driven along the Mediterranean coast with incredible vistas, arriving an hour later at a spacious country home with its own generous slice of beach. The limo hadn't even stopped when Lauro came flying through the front entrance to latch onto Concepción as she stepped out, nearly knocking her back into the car. Only Franz's hands on her backside prevented that. Lauro was a different kid than the one rescued from the cave.

"He sometimes awakes in the night with a scream," his mother explained later as we took to the patio, "but we take him to our bed between us so that he knows he is safe. He plays and laughs again, but he does not let us out of his sight."

"He will come to know he is safe here. We have the Carabinieri here all the time. They watch him closely when he is not with us," Señor Guzzanti explained. I thought about the insecurity the world had inherited.

That afternoon was spent with the last vestiges of tension melting into oblivion. Even my self-consciousness of wearing a European-style bikini evaporated. Lauro, Concepción, Alejandro, and I frolicked without care as the adults sat beneath umbrellas to talk and laugh at our antics. Taking a breather, Franz and Concepción stretched out on beach towels to chat and further dilute his white body with some honest tan while Alejandro, Lauro, and I filled the air with kites and beaching waves with wake boards.

I was amazed at little guy's resiliency. In such a short time Lauro popped out from behind his defensive wall. The silver chain and crucifix bounced wildly as his small, brown body ran and twirled bouncing circles along the edge of the surf, feet flying without care as he ran to jump on the board, laughing, and falling on his backside with a splash. Once dull, somber eyes now sparkled with joy, laughter tumbled freely from a face-splitting grin. The petite ten-year-old who's brown eyes were perpetually swollen and red from crying, who cringed, and clung at the drop of a pin, now displayed no worries, not even caring if his loose bikini would stay on. The terrible nightmare was over and put away.

We extended our stay one day to enjoy that special time then came a farewell dinner with as many courses as when Grandma and I were guests at the El Hierro Governor's Palace. There were a number of people there, some of northern Italy's most noted personalities. Fortunately, at our suggestion, they brought their daughters and included dancing. Alejandro and I were in Ligurian heaven.

As the festivities tapered down, I stepped out onto the veranda for some cool air. Off to one end of the huge balcony, Franz and Concepción were saying farewell as his flight to Strasbourg left quite early in the morning where his mother would meet him. That's where both he and she would be living. Apparently, there was more than just a rift between father and son.

I was about to walk up and say goodbye, Concepción reached up, took him by the shoulders, pulled his head down, and engaged him a monumental lip lock that curled my toes as happened back in the cave just watching them. And, it wasn't a short kiss, either. At first, his arms stretched out sideways from his body and flapped as if trying to fly before slowly encircling my sister as their heads did slow gyrations. It seemed an eternity before they came up for air whereupon she backed up, still holding both his hands, said "Goodbye," and walked away.

At the Guzzanti estate we took a little time to lay out plans to document the terror those people caused. The problem was that revealing the facts would embarrass some good people. Señor Guzzanti agree that the truth about these people should be made known, but how? I then remembered the writer we met on El Hierro who helped with our first book last year. His suggestion was perfect.

"How about telling it as a fictional novel "based on true events," he said. "I haven't time in my schedule, but I know a good writer who might take it on, if you can put up with an old curmudgeon Celt. He can spin quite a tale."

A phone call got him out of bed. We forgot the time difference between Italy and Nevada until it dawned on Grandma who gasped.

"It's only 1:30 a.m. here. I work late. Haven't even thought about bed, yet."

Fearful of the warning that he was the grumpy sort, it was mostly a joke, although when we started making it into a movie two years later, he definitely became a curmudgeon about Hollywood's "artistic" changes. I think it was over something about adding a sex scene in the cave. Fortunately, they had to deal with him and not Grandma.

Bidding a final farewell to our gracious hosts, the five of us climbed aboard a chartered Dassault Falcon 900EX back to El Hierro. This super comfortable air beast even came with a flight attendant, giving Grandma a different perspective on charter flying as we arrived home in three and a half hours. You could see the calculations running through her head. True, a lot more expensive, but the grueling commercial flight between Valverde and Lincoln could be cut from twenty-seven hours to nine.

We spoke little to one other until sighting Gibraltar, and then Concepción plopped down in the seat next to mine. "You've been unusually quiet," she said.

"Just had some things on my mind."

"Are you jealous?"

"Huh?"

"That I kissed Franz?"

"You knew I was there?"

"I spotted you trying to be very discrete as I left."

"I wasn't spying, really. I just came out for some air. Besides, kissing guys is your business. It's not my place to say with who or how." I have to be honest, there was some jealousy itching the back of my head.

"It really meant nothing. I mean, there is nothing between Franz and I."

"I didn't think there would be. Gay guys don't

usually get with girls except socially, maybe, but from an outsider's view it sure looked serious."

"I really wondered about the things he said about himself. That was just something for him to think about."

"You do that to people all the time."

"What do you mean?"

"Last year you told Alejandro about all the girls seeing him swimming naked to teach him a lesson about modesty. This year you had Kessare talk to me. He listened. I didn't. Now you set Franz to re-evaluate his sex life. I wonder who's next. My guess is that you're going to become the world's premier advice columnist."

Concepción tossed me a startled look, got up, and moved to another seat. I sat a moment listening to the hum of the engines, staring out at a thin bank of clouds over North Africa before getting up and moving toward the front where Grandma and Papa were playing Hearts. I watched until the two competitive players finished the game.

"I'm worried," I said, laying my problem on the table.

"About what, dear?" Grandma asked.

"Capt. Santana. His great, great, well, way back grandfather was a crewman aboard the Raven. He was a really big help."

"Yes," Grandma said with a displeased tone. "I'd like to talk to him about that."

"He should have stopped you two," Papa said, adding his displeasure.

"Not likely. If he hadn't helped, we'd have

found someone else and who knows what help they would have been. Alejandro and I had set our course whatever might come."

"You have the Dolephene stubborn streak," Grandma grunted.

"Who were Evreux's, and it's not stubborn. It's determination. Anyway, we owe him a lot."

"How much did you offer him?" Pappa asked.

"He wouldn't take money. Said it was payment for a debt long overdue. I think the Captain saved the first Santana or something. I'll have to check that out in the Captain's journal. Anyway, I'd like to see that Capt. Santana stays out of trouble."

"What do you have in mind?" Grandma asked.

"He does a little smuggling on the side to sort of make ends meet. I'd like to see he gets $100K a year, so he can quit."

They both choked.

"You do realize, Francis," Grandma said after recovering, "To give a person that kind of money is like giving a diabetic a bowl of sugar to eat."

"You might be right. What do you suggest?"

"Perhaps something a little less dangerous."

"You may be right. Let's do $50K with the stipulation he must retire from all elicit activity or forfeit the stipend."

Grandma and Papa looked at one another for a time before agreeing.

"There's another matter. Franz. He wants to become an Anthropologist. Even if his father coughed up the money, which I seriously doubt, he wouldn't accept it. I'd like to see him receive a scholarship to the best school for that."

"That seems appropriate. I'll look into such schools," Grandma said.

"Another thing. I don't want him to know where the money is coming from."

"I'll talk to Señor Montoya. He may be able to help with that. Anything else?"

"No."

"You're feeling like such a philanthropist. What about Lauro?"

"His pappa is well off. I don't think I can help there, except, maybe we could fly them to Casa de St. Nazaire next summer."

"Excellent idea. Anything else?"

"No. Well, maybe. The head of the De Stefano family. Could we hire a hit man . . .?"

"Absolutely not, young man," Grandma scolded until seeing the twinkle in my eyes. "But we might be able to encourage the authorities to put more pressure on them," she suggested as a wicked smile tweaked the edges of her lips.

Chapter 18

R & R Reunion

Arriving in Valverde, we stayed at Aunt Herminia's overnight before heading to the hacienda. With that, life generally returned as it had been, before all the extracurricular episodes. Becoming almost inseparable, my brother, and sister, and I explored the island both above and below ground. We had a real curiosity about the network of caverns below the hacienda and made some startling discoveries. Of course, we spent lots of time at Dolphin Cove. The primitive, one-room hut was now a rustic, two-room cabin with modern facilities. At least once a week we shut down the disco. Well, maybe twice a week, but no more. I wanted to spend chaperoned outings with Isabella. However, she worked it, neither of her parents was completely aware of her involvement in our rescue.

Three weeks before returning to Nebraska and school, Franz and his mother arrived to work on the book Grandma proposed.

"I have developed a liking for the sun," he said, now sporting some healthy-looking color.

The writer we engaged sent an older lady with a gorgeous, thick pile of white hair to gather the necessary information. I could see why. She was talented and very good at uncovering details we might not have considered. As previously decided, Lauro would not be involved. Triggering a childhood defense, he locked away those frightening weeks in captivity, and his parents were not amenable to opening that door. Perhaps not the most healthy approach according to psychologists, but it helped him get on with being a child again, at least for the few years that remained of such a wonderfully carefree time.

On the other hand, Franz had an amazing memory for detail. He was there when Lauro arrived. They spoke at first, and he remembered those details before the boy retreated into a protective shell. He also revealed things Concepción had not noticed, keeping the lady scratching furiously on a pad.

Franz also became an instant hit at the disco. Oh sure, he danced with girls, but he also danced with Rami Rasheed, the jeweler. On the public beach, he became a flower as girls swarmed around him. That was understandable. Whether casually attired or in a bikini he had regained the lost weight and reacquired the physique girls are attracted to. Tall at 6-2, his 190 pound frame was hard, and tanned. Slightly cherry-tinted blond hair swept off his head in large ocean-like waves curling tightly mid-neck. Dark eyebrows hovered over captivating, bright, green eyes. The generous mouth seemed perpetually spread into a warming smile.

Unlike me, the first time associating with girls, he was comfortable having them around. They posed neither threat, challenge, nor the physical stimulant we heterosexual teens constantly struggle with. Open about his gayness, he posed no threat to them and actually garnered more attention.

Sitting on the family patio rehearsing our day at the beach, his mother said, "I like very much der change I see. Meine son hat always been reclusive. Now he has friends. They are nice boys, too."

"I war well back in der closet," he quipped.

"Well, I like you out." Sitting at his side, she reached an arm around his shoulders and hugged him.

Since the harrowing escape, he embarked on a new life, coping with personal challenges, gradually becoming laid back, easing into the more outgoing lifestyle. He had become comfortable with whom he was and no longer ashamed to walk down the street or along the incoming waves holding another man's hand, or even kissing him in public.

After returning to the hacienda, I quickly fell into a routine similar to that of my ancestor. As their part of resurrecting the estate, Alejandro and Concepción restored the garden between the house and stream that had been vital to Casa de St. Nazaire's founders. During our absence, the weeds had gotten the upper hand. Reclamation took three, very long mornings, then only shorter daily cultivating to maintain its productivity. This is where Franz found me at six the first morning after he arrived.

"You do this every day?" he asked, leaning on the fence.

"I do now. My great grandfather lots of times removed came every day, rain or shine, when he was here, otherwise it was up to his wife, Mariah, and later their children. When he first arrived, it was necessary to come every day for survival. After becoming prosperous and could afford to hire someone to do the weeding, he continued. I wondered why, but now understand. It's so beautiful and peaceful in the mornings. My mind seems to clear. I really feel like tackling the day after putting up the hoe."

By the time Grandma called us for breakfast at 7:30 Franz had shed sandals and socks and buried his feet in the rich soil. Washing hands and feet at the kitchen door, she amply rewarded us with heaping plates of bacon, scrambled eggs with goat cheese, toast, and glasses of cold milk, all from the plantation.

Not accustomed to doing his own dishes, he pitched in with cleanup after which we sat on the veranda with the writer's assistant. Like me, he remained barefoot, as sandals were not necessary, except for the hikes to the cove, although several months later he wrote they were necessary when winter's cold blanketed Germany – at least out-doors.

The atmosphere was serene, but two hours of intensive grilling was exhausting – for her – so after lunch Franz and I decided to amble down to Dol-phin Cove, while she labored over a laptop. Of course, stopping at the hot pool was almost man-datory.

Sitting chest-deep in the water, he took a deep breath, threw his head back, and sighed. "Oh, this is so nice, to truly be alone. No paparazzi sneaking around taking pictures or inventing lies." He laughed then cast about. "They do not come up here?"

"No. The police are relatives. They keep a close eye on any that show up and harass them until they leave, or they find themselves escorted off is-land. Actually, not many come any more. For all they know I'm just the kid that found all that pirate treasure and that's old news. They don't know about Italy . . . yet."

"That will change."

"I suppose. I'm not going to worry about it. So, how are you dealing with it?"

"It ist difficult at times to find privacy. It seems there ist always one or two lurking in der forest when I go for daily run. Sometimes I regret going public, but then think how good it has felt to dis-credit der man who was ein samenspender."

I didn't pursue that issue. I knew he was extremely bitter and I couldn't judge him on that issue. It's hard to know how one would feel in those circumstances.

"Der media thought to really have something about meine being gay."

"What'd you do?"

"I war on syndicated talk program. The host asked me. I leaned back, stretched meine arms along der back of der sofa, looked him straight in der eye, and said, 'Ja, I am homosexual. That ist why people like meine mutter's man are afraid of me. It challenges their masculinity. I am liberated from all that nonsense."

Then the host asked, "You are frequently seen in der company of many beautiful women. Ist that to cover your homosexual tendencies?"

"What ist to cover?" I countered. "I have made no attempt to hide what ist true. That has been public information since meine escape from der Italian gangsters. Women are very nice, so compassionate, understanding, intelligent, so mentally stimulating. Heterosexuals like yourself look at them as objects of sex, fight für superiority over other desiring men, and demean them. I look at women as equals.

"You should have heard der audience response. They have great difficulty controlling der applause. To counter meine frankness der scandalists made up crude und debasing stories of meine trysts with other men. They even hinted that I violated Lauro."

"Geez! What'd you do with that?" I asked.

"I say to them, bring forward any man or boy who can show that I have sexual relations mit them, or as der minister say in der wedding ceremony, '*halten Sie für immer Ihren Frieden*,' hold for good your peace.' Naturally, they could not. Oh, they thought to fabricate something, but were caught in their lies und disgraced. You see, I war always too shy to do such things."

"And now? You've changed," I asked.

"Ja, I have changed, thanks to your encouragement. I have learned to, as you say, to lay back und take life one day at a time, und enjoy every minute. I go to disco and espressohaus und have fun mit new friends." He blushed and giggled softly. "When go to Strasbourg I walk in der forest mit meine uncle. We have long talk. He ist wise man. He believes each of us are what we are, there ist no changing that. We can hide it, force our real self out of sight, but must deal mit it coming to der surface throughout life. I decide to not fight and live mit who I am. I become honest mit meineself. I can face these people."

"So, when the time comes and you meet the right man, will you marry?"

"Will you be my best man?"

"Sure, if you ask."

"Ah, David, that ist what I like about you," he laughed. "Creatures like me do not intimidate you."

"You are not a creature! You are a good human being," I protested angrily.

"Danke," he replied after a short silence and then said quietly, "You also. I have decided to be what I am. If I find a gūt person, perhaps I will marry, but sometimes think maybe I will be celibate."

"That would to be a tough road. I know a Catholic priest back home, a teacher in my school. He took a vow of celibacy. There were all those revelations others of his religion were not successful keeping their vow. He admitted praying every morning and night to overcome the desires of the flesh. He says it is incredibly difficult."

"It ist matter for person to decide what controls one's life, der mind or der body."

"Someone I know said something very similar. I learning that doing life right won't be as easy as I so naively thought."

Stepping out to stand under the cold stream, Franz cut loose a loud whistled as one might at a girl. Whipping around, I stared at him.

"Sie haben einen schönen hintern. You have nice butt," he said, then started laughing so hard to slip off the submerged rock he was sitting on. I turned all sorts of red shades. "Now you know what it ist like for a girl," he finally managed to say.

"Did Concepción put you up to that?!"

His grin was incriminating proof, but a lesson well taken. I had never whistled at a girl in that way, not that I wasn't tempted, but hadn't so far. From that day forward, I may have had good reason to start puckering up, but remembered that lesson about respect.

At the dragon's head we stood side by side peering down at the black shapes slicing back and forth in the water. He stepped back and shuddered. I knew the feeling. Stripping down to my bikini, he stared in disbelief at what I might be up to.

"It's a whole new life. Are you a man or a mouse," I challenged, getting into position at the small cairn of rocks, which was the starting point for the leap.

"According to some, neither."

"Just land feet first," I said giving my all and disappearing over the edge with a long and loud, "Yahoo."

I was splashing with the dolphins when he came off, one extended dive bomber scream. There was no keeping him from repeating the feat except becoming worn out from running back up the steep trail to the top.

The evening before his return to Germany two weeks later, we were lounging in the courtyard after a day in Valverde celebrating another local holiday. I could tell there was something he wanted to say or do, but not when others were around. Finally, we had a few minutes alone when his mother and Grandma went upstairs to finish packing. There was a box about eighteen inches square setting on a long, narrow console table next to the entry hall. Retrieving it, he handed me the box, and sat, watching expectantly. Pulling off the wrapping paper, I stared inside and began to laugh, and withdrew a whip.

"Hey, anyone here?" Alejandro called out as he came in the front door. Seeing us, he came back. "Whoa! A whip. This is really nice," he said, inspecting it carefully.

"My uncle works leather as hobby. He showed me how to make it," Franz said.

"I will cherish it as well as the memory. Thanks, Franz."

"Oh, I almost forgot," Alejandro said, handing me the whip and reaching inside his shirt. "A letter came for you today," and handed it to Franz.

"A letter? Für me? Here?"

"Must be important. Cousin Gonzales brought it to the museum as soon as he arrived with the mail from Tenerife. It's marked urgent."

Franz tore it open. As he read, the dark tan he'd acquired melted as his mouth dropped open. I knew what it was. Papa Montoya called the day before.

"What is it?" Alejandro asked, concerned it might be bad news.

"Ist from meine uncle in Strasbourg. Ist copy of letter he received two days ago. It says an anonymous person in Berlin read about meine ordeal and war impressed. He has arranged für me to study anthropology . . . at University of Western Florida . . . in der United States!"

A lump came to my throat as the big German began to cry. After becoming estranged from his wealthy father, he arranged to begin working as a restaurant waiter after the European August vacation period to earn money so to attend one of the less expensive German schools, giving up the dream of becoming an anthropologist. Suddenly, Franz found himself heading for one of the most prestigious schools in the world for that degree. He was totally overwhelmed.

Nine years later, Dr. Franz Zeiler (he changed his name to that of his mother's family) stood on the brink of a great career having completed studies in Historical Anthropology and Maritime Archeology. He never knew his benefactor and patron, just as I wanted.

As for Capt. Santana, the rapscallion continued to ply the Mediterranean taking legitimate charters, no longer engaging in dangerous, extra-curricular activities. I kept in touch, and along with my brother and sister, went on extended charters for a few more commando lessons. His only regret was missing some of the excitement of smuggling. However, we saw to that some years later. Retiring from charters, he embarked on a career with more excitement than he ever thought possible.

What was intended to be a carefree, relaxing summer had supernovaed into a billion pieces. After the research lady returned home, Grandma and I did enjoy some respite at Casa de St. Nazaire, settling into a quieter life insulated from the prying eyes of the world. We even managed that for a time after returning to Nebraska. Eventually, it came out that Concepción had been one of the children rescued from the gangsters, and that linked me to the story.

We continued to embellish the roles played by the Italian police and military for diplomatic reasons. Besides, there were friendships and contacts in that country we didn't want broken. However, finding peace again became a 24/7 chore as the press periodically hounded us. Only little Lauro was able to slip into peaceful obscurity – until becoming an adult.

Epilogue

"My great, great, great gran come by yo bones as young girl. Very rare. Very powerful," Momma Bearbear explained.

With his nose practically inside the metal box, upon hearing that the contents once belong to a living person, Delfin's face screwed up as he backed away, normal curiosity dampened.

"Yeah," I said over the top of Matthew Barber's journal which I was reading. "Most folk object to giving up their fingers."

"Oh, dey not mind when dey be dead," Momma said with a wry smile

"How do they work?" Concepción asked.

"I pours dem out on table and dey tell a story. But as I say, these are very special bones. Dey not tell what is to be. Dey tell what has been. See here, there be eight bones, one for each of de pirate friends, Aloysius Shaver, his son Matthew Barber, he de maker of our clan, Margaret DuBris, Lawrence Merryfield, Harvey Gibbs, Lawrence Pennington, and your ancestor, François Evreux.

"Remember de prophecy say that in day to come all de pirate friends will become one. The bones tell when de blood of one mixes with another. When dat happen, dey do not scatter to lay alone, but come together as one."

"So what happens when all the bones come together?" Delfin asked as his curiosity overcame initial revulsion and returned to examine them again, from a slightly further position.

"Prophecy say when blood of all de friends unite a great leader will rise up for all family, a king, " Momma Bearbear answered, her voice crescendoing in pitch and volume before suddenly dropping into a silence that allowed the words to ring and echo in our ears.

"Can I see them work?" Delfin said.

Momma looked at the boy a moment, and then at Concepción, and finally at me. My eyes were no longer decrypting the old English writing, instead looking over the top of Matthew's journal.

She began a haunting, sing-song chant in a language I had never heard as her dark eyes glazed over. A chill began to run along my backbone as goose bumps popped up everywhere. After weaving long fingers over the can of bones in an intricate pattern, she quite unexpectedly inverted the contents onto the dining table. In deathly silence, we stared as she slowly lifted the can to expose the whitish bones. They formed one, unified mass.

"It has come to pass!" she cried, tears beginning to stream down her coppery face. "All their blood now flows in one!"

"Who is it?" Delfin shouted.

The answer is in

A Pirate's Legacy: The Bones

Coming in the fall of 2012

" . . . this funny and suspenseful novel sets itself apart." -
Carlie Helfinger

Sean O'Mordha

CIC: The Canary Island Commandos is
Sean's third book in the A Pirate's Legacy series chronicling the lives and in-
teractions of the 15th Century pirate, François Evreux (The Dolphin)
and his 21st Century descendant, David Dolephene.

"The author certainly has a finger on the teenager's pulse." -
Jackson Trowbridge

He is also the author of Death by Top Secret, Incident at Beaver
Creek, and For All Time and Eternity: Waters From the Deep, Man
With No Name, and numerous short stories.

For more information see Sean's website at

www.oldguey.webs.com.